FRAMED!

FRAMED!

Canada's Great Northern Prison
(The Worlds Prison For Terrorists)

DALE CAHOON

authorHOUSE®

AuthorHouse™
1663 Liberty Drive
Bloomington, IN 47403
www.authorhouse.com
Phone: 1-800-839-8640

© 2013 by Dale Cahoon. All rights reserved.
Edited by Kenneth D. Cahoon

No part of this book may be reproduced, stored in a retrieval system, or transmitted by any means without the written permission of the author.

Published by AuthorHouse   05/16/2013

ISBN: 978-1-4817-5332-6 (sc)
ISBN: 978-1-4817-5331-9 (e)

Library of Congress Control Number: 2013908927

Any people depicted in stock imagery provided by Thinkstock are models, and such images are being used for illustrative purposes only.
Certain stock imagery © Thinkstock.

This book is printed on acid-free paper.

Because of the dynamic nature of the Internet, any web addresses or links contained in this book may have changed since publication and may no longer be valid. The views expressed in this work are solely those of the author and do not necessarily reflect the views of the publisher, and the publisher hereby disclaims any responsibility for them.

CONTENTS

My Story 1
The Day My Life Changed 8
Back At Great Northern Prison 24
Planning The Escape 31
The Escape 37
Back In New York 43
Collecting The Facts 47
My First Break 54
Finding Selene 61
Tim's Return 68
Recruiting Selene 72
Recruiting Lisa 79
The Embassy Escape 88
Dr. Walkers Secret 105
The Real Estate Scam 111
The Interrogations 119
The Seduction 130
The News Conference 135
They've Found Us! 139
We've Been Compromised! 142
The Safe House 147
Finding Randy 157
The Hearing 173

Epilogue (One Year Later) 197
AS For The Cast Of Characters 199

Spring 2013: "As warden of the world's first international maximum security Prison, I welcome you. Great Northern has been built unlike any other prison in the world," he continued. No fences, no gates, and yet no possible escape. We are over 1000 miles from any kind of civilization in the great Canadian North West Territories tundra."

"We are assembling here, over 1500 of the worst of the worst criminals in the world. You are convicted murderers, child molesters, rapists, and terrorists," he said, looking down at us from his office balcony two stories above us. "Let me assure you that no one knows you're where you are, and they probably never will." "This is the last place you will ever see because every one of you is a lifer with almost no chance of parole or freedom," he continued. "We have represented at this institution people from forty seven countries so far."

"You probably noticed that there are no wire fences or high walls. There are no armed guards to stop you from leaving. You are free to leave at anytime and if the freezing weather in the winter or the soft muskeg in the summer doesn't kill you the wolves will. There are no roads or trails, just a landing strip to bring you to this forsaken hole."

"Inside the prison you will notice there are no cells, no chains and very few guards. We do have some nice amenities like a gymnasium, big screen T.V.'s, weight rooms, cafeteria, library, swimming pool and several other things that can make your time here pass nicely."

There is however a catch. Starting today, for you new arrivals, you will be given some privilege points. One hundred points to be precise. Each day that you maintain that level, you will be able to use any of our modern facilities. Each day of good behavior will be rewarded with one privilege point. However, if you drop below that 100 point mark you will be placed in solitary confinement until you earn back your points."

"Let me give you some examples of how to lose points. 1. Start or be involved in any kind of a physical confrontation with a fellow prisoner. That will cost you 10 points. 2. If you do not keep your area clean it will cost you 5 points. 3. If you destroy any of our property you will lose 10 points. 4. Fail to do your assigned chores and you will lose 5 points and still have to do those chores. 5. Verbally or physically abuse any of the staff and you lose 25 points. Let me make this very clear, behave yourself and you will be treated with respect, drop below the minimum standard and I promise, you will regret being here! A person in solitary has no privileges, none. Each point lost will cost you 1 day in confinement. We have a zero tolerance policy."

"This prison is equipped with the best in electronic surveillance equipment. We see and record everything you do every day. So let's try and be on our best behavior and we will get along just fine. Now follow your leaders to the check in area and get your assignments. Oh, and by the way this is a no smoking and no alcohol facility, except in designated areas. We have some staff on hand to help you with addictions. You will now be escorted by your guards and register for your stay with us. Wait for your name to be called and enter the door straight in front of you."

MY STORY

My name is Phillip Chambers and I am one of the early ones to arrive here in the great white north. My saga began only a few months earlier. I have been convicted of murder in the first degree and a sponsor of terrorism and I am innocent! Here is my story!

I'm 24 years old. I am 6'2" tall and played outside linebacker for four years while in school. That was a nice way to make it through college without a great deal of debt. I have remained in pretty good shape, working out at least three days a week. I have black hair, had the name dreamboat in college and I am single. I graduated from Harvard law school a short while ago and secured a job with the law firm of Foreman, Hudson and Zakarai. I was surprised they recruited me so hard but was thrilled that they did because the money was so good for a first year lawyer. I hoped that some of their reasoning came from a background check which showed me as a student who was never in trouble and could be trustworthy and counted on to be loyal.

Foreman was a small office and this company specialized in overseas marketing with a major interest in foreign oil. My job quickly evolved from a desk clerk to working with my mentor, Mr. Zakarai (from now on

I will refer to him as MR. Z) on several sensitive and secretive projects. Little did I know that my trust of the company, my employer and my associates would take me on a whirlwind ride across the ocean to Middle East countries and eventually to this forsaken wilderness and away from those who I love and care for most.

I received an assignment, in 2012, to accompany MR. Z to Dubai as his assistant. I was told virtually nothing concerning the trip and was advised I would be briefed once we arrived in the United Arab Emirates. From the minute we arrived I couldn't help but notice the elegance and grandeur of this tiny country. We entered the hotel and I stood beside my boss as he arranged for my room. I was surprised that the hotel clerk recognized him and called him by name. Obviously he had been here" many times." Here is your key and your expense card," Mr. Z said. "Enjoy your stay and don't worry about the card limit." There isn't one," he smiled. My hotel suite was elegant and looked over the harbor and the Palms. I was told by MR. Z that I would be contacted by someone later that afternoon and he would update me on what my assignment would be. He told me to follow instructions, complete my assignment, and he would meet me for dinner that night in the executive dining room.

My family always had money when I was growing up. My Father was a banker with a business degree which was also from Harvard. I never really wanted for anything growing up but being here with an unlimited budget was completely new to me.

I showered, got changed and turned on the television. There was CNN news and it was just like being home. I relaxed and took a short nap until it was interrupted by a knock at the door. I opened it to find one of the most beautiful women I had ever seen in my life." My name is Selene," she said." May I come in? she asked. "Of course", I said, holding the door open for her." She was carrying a brief case which she set on the coffee table as she sat on the chair in the room. I couldn't help noticing that her briefcase was exactly like the one I had brought with me. I asked her if she would like something to drink and she said, No thank you." I couldn't help notice the sky blue outfit she was wearing. Her long black hair was past her shoulders and her blue eyes seemed to look right through me.

"Mr. Chambers, I was told to deliver this package to you and ask if you, in turn, would deliver it to an associate of Mr. Z's on his behalf. The combination lock number is 61854," she continued. "Please memorize it and do not write it down anywhere." "No problem," I said. "Can you give me some instructions on where to take it?" I asked. She reached into her shoulder bag and handed me a small machine. When she gave it to me I instantly recognized it as a mini GPS. "You need to leave in exactly one hour," she said. "A cab will be waiting for you. It will be marked number 32. Get in and direct the driver to the drop off point following the instructions on your GPS. Please make sure you have the driver start with three consecutive right turns to be sure you are not being followed. "O.K.," I replied, not understanding the secrecy that seemed to exist.

"As you arrive at your destination you will see a sign that says Europo's. Please enter the door directly under the sign. Go in and sit down at the table in the very back of the café," she said. "Someone will contact you in a few minutes and ask you if you would like to select a wine from the cellar," she continued. "Say yes and follow his lead. If no one contacts you for ten minutes, please leave immediately and return to the hotel." Remember," she concluded. "Once you are inside the wine cellar, you will be asked for the briefcase. Ask him who wants it," and if he says" Riker" then give it to him. He in turn will give you a bottle of wine in a brown paper bag. Take it and leave for your hotel immediately."

3

"Do you think you can do that?" she asked." I think I can handle it," I smiled back at her. "In that case I will leave this case in your care. Remember, if you feel anyone is following you please return to the hotel and come back to your room". "OK," I said, a bit puzzled by the secrecy of the entire affair," I'll get it done." "Mr. Z has a lot of confidence in you, she said as she stood and headed for the door. "I hope we will meet again in a less formal situation" she said as I opened the door for her. "I am certainly looking forward to that I replied." With that she walked down the corridor and around the corner and was gone. The aroma of her perfume was still in the air as I returned to my sofa. It was very intoxicating and an aroma I had never smelled before. I had had several relationships in my life but I can honestly say this was the most beautiful woman I had ever seen in my life.

What is so secretive about all of this? I thought to myself. I felt more like Tom Cruise in Mission Impossible than a small time lawyer from New York. However I knew that MR. Z had complete trust in me and that was enough for now. I sat looking at the briefcase and my curiosity got the best of me. The woman had not said not to open it so I pretended that doing so would be of no harm." Oh my," I thought, "What was that combination and why had she told me that number if she didn't want me to open it? My dad is sixty one my grandma is just over eighty five and I had intercepted four passes in college." 61854," I thought to myself. "Wow, are you ever smart."

I reached down and began to move the tumblers. Once they fell into place I lifted the top of the case. Inside was nothing but a small alloy flask. It was about three inches long and seemed to have something solid concealed inside. Also inside was a sealed envelope. I picked them both up and then put them gently back to their original positions. That was enough for me. I closed the case and placed it back on the coffee table. I turned the T.V. back on and waited for the time I was to leave.

Time moved slowly as I awaited my exit from the room. I couldn't get the thought of Selene out of my head, partly because I could still smell her scent. "Get her out of your head," I thought to myself. "You'll probably never see her again, and besides that she is completely out of your league." I waited a few more minutes and then headed for the lobby. Just as I walked out of my hotel a cab pulled up. I instantly noticed number thirty two on the top and opened the door and got in.

"Where to sir?" came the driver's voice in broken English. "Just follow my directions as we go I said. "Turn right here, followed by turn right again," just as the GPS indicated. It only took about ten minutes before the cab pulled up in front of the café. "Wait for me" I said to the cab driver. "I'll only be a few minutes." I exited the cab and headed for the front door. As I walked in I was greeted with a small wave from the man behind the bar. "Sit wherever you like Sir, we will be with you shortly." "Thank you," I replied and moved to the back of the café. The place was very nice and music was playing softly in the background.

In a couple of minutes a man, dressed as a server, approached my table and asked, "Would you care to choose a wine from our wine cellar?" Yes I would, I replied as I stood and followed him through the door. We walked down the hallway and then down a long set of stairs to the basement and into the wine cellar. We continued past the racks of wine and then up to another door. The waiter knocked twice and I heard the lock open on the other side. Once again I followed the waiter into the room.

Sitting directly in front of me was a middle eastern man dressed in a white suit. He looked about 5'8" overweight but gave the air of upper class. He was balding on top and I could tell he was the one in charge. He motioned to me and as I moved forward he said, "May I have that briefcase please?" "May I ask who wants it?" I asked as I had been coached? "My name is Riker" he replied, extending his hand as he rose from his chair. I shook his hand and he told me to have a seat. There were two other men in the room and they stood directly behind Riker with their arms folded over their chests. They looked like body guards and I could tell by looking at one of them that he had a holster under his sports coat. I placed the briefcase on the desk and pushed it towards him.

"Thank you for bringing this to me Mr. Chambers," said the man. "I know this may seem fairly mysterious to you, but the enclosed documents are of vital importance. Will you please give me the combination?" he asked. "Sure it's 61854," I replied. He opened the case and without removing anything from it, closed it back up and said, "everything seems to be in order," Thanks again for bringing it to me. You are free to leave," he continued. "My waiter will escort you to back to the dining room." I followed the man back up the stairs and into the café. "Mr. Z asked me to give you this bottle of wine and take it back to the United States for him. It is his favorite white wine and I assured him you would deliver it for him."

Number thirty was still waiting as I exited the café. I got in and said "take me back to the hotel please." "Yes Sir" he responded and drove away. We arrived shortly and I headed for my suite immediately, carrying the wine tightly under my arm. It was dusk as I arrived at my room. As I opened the door I noticed an envelope on the floor that had been slipped under the door. I opened it and found my return ticket to New York, which was scheduled to leave the next afternoon.

I picked up my phone and called the restaurant just beside main lobby. "Hello," came an answer, "how may I help you?" "I was just wondering if you could tell me what time Mr. Zakari's reservation was made?" "Just one moment and I will check for you," he responded. In a couple of minutes he returned and said, "I'm sorry sir but we have no one by that name with a reservation tonight," came the reply. "Is there more than one restaurant in the hotel?". I asked. "Yes but it would still be in our data base if anyone by that name had made a reservation." "Thank you," I said. "I will check with you later," and hung up the phone.

I picked up the receiver and pushed zero for the front desk. "Good evening Mr. Chambers what can we do for you this evening?" asked the operator. "Could you connect me with Mr. Zakari?" I asked. "Do you know his room number Sir?" she asked. "No, but he arrived with me earlier today." There was a short pause and then she answered, "I'm sorry but we have no record of a Mr. Zakari registered at the hotel." "That's impossible" I replied. "We checked in together just this afternoon." "I apologize but I have no record of him at our hotel Sir," she concluded. "Thank" you I said. and hung up the phone.

By now I was beginning to feel some stress but at the same time I was starving. I looked at the room service menu and decided I would eat in my room and go to bed early. I had slept a bit on the all nighter to Dubai and hadn't eaten anything but the fruit basket I had found in my room upon my arrival. I turned the TV back on and watched the news and waited for my dinner to arrive. About twenty minutes later there was a knock at my door and a voice that said "room service." I opened the door and took the food from the bell hop. Little did I know that it the last meal I would have in a very long time.

7

THE DAY MY LIFE CHANGED

The next morning I awoke to the sounds of police and fire sirens. Not just a couple but a steady stream of them. I looked out my window and saw a fire blaze about a mile down the road from the hotel. I turned the T.V. on and the same news was everywhere. I watched in horror as I realized there had been a bombing. It was at the home of the Kuwait ambassador to the U.E.A. It looked to me like this once safe haven was now on the terrorist list as well.

I watched intently wanting to get more details on the bombing. Within the next fifteen minutes it was confirmed that the Ambassador, his wife, a number of aids and two UEA enforcement officers had been killed and other embassy workers were still missing.

Once again I picked up the phone and asked the whereabouts of my boss Mr. Z. Again the message came back that no Mr. Z. had even registered at the hotel. I must admit that many thoughts were racing through my mind. I reached into my briefcase and picked up my cell phone. I turned it on and tried to call back to our New York office. There was no service so I grabbed the room phone, gave the operator the office number and asked her to put me through. I waited and she came back on the line. "I'm sorry Sir, but that number is no longer in service," she said. Getting more upset by the minute I asked her to try again and again I received the same answer. What is going on I thought to myself, can this really be happening?

I decided to get my things packed and get to the airport. My only desire was to get out of this place. More reports were coming in on CNN as I packed my bag. I remembered to put the wine in my suitcase to take back to Mr. Z, that is if I could ever find him again. I knew that getting to the airport would be a problem with the mass confusion outside. I finished packing and headed out the door and down to the lobby. The hotel was buzzing as I exited the elevator. I headed to the desk to check out.

I waited a few minutes in line and then approached the clerk at the desk. "Checkout for room 2414 I," said. "Thank you Mr. Chambers, she said taking my card. A moment later she handed me back my card and said, "your room has already been paid for" She continued. "I hope you enjoyed your stay with us." I nodded yes, took my card and headed to the hotel doors.

I was surprised to find a cab waiting out front. I got in and the cabbie said, "where to Sir?" "To the airport," I said "I need terminal B." When I arrived at the airport it was teeming with people. I paid for my cab and entered the terminal pulling my suitcase and holding my briefcase. There was airport security everywhere. I approached the boarding desk. Even though I was very early, I could see I wasn't the only one in a hurry to get out of there. I handed the clerk my ticket and gave him my bag to check through for me. He handed me back my boarding pass and said, "There is a delay on all flights right now, so please take a seat and we will let you know when we are ready to board the plane."

I walked over to a booth near the waiting area and got myself a muffin and some milk and then returned to my seat. Once again I tried to use my cell phone but I had no reception. I must have dozed off for a time and was startled when I heard my name. I opened my eyes to see two security officers in uniform standing before me.

"Are you Mr. Philip Chambers?" one of the men asked me. "Uh, yes I am" I replied "is there something wrong?" "You need to come with me" the officer said in a stern voice. "OK" I said, "where are we going?" I asked. "Just follow me," he replied. "Is this your briefcase?" he asked. "Yes it is." I said as I glanced down at it. The other security officer picked it up and began to walk off. I stood and followed him and was trailed by the other officer. We walked down a long corridor and then down a flight of stairs until I saw a sign that said Security. The lead man opened the door and motioned me inside. The room was fairly large but only had two chairs and a desk.

"Wait here" the officer said, Someone will be with you shortly. Before I go I will need to see your passport, your papers and your wallet." I said "Sure" and reached inside my suit coat and produced both of them. They took them and headed for the door. By now my head was really swimming but nothing could prepare for what was to follow.

I sat in the room for what seemed to be forever. I glanced at my watch and thought to myself, "it's a good thing I got here early." There was still over an hour until my flight was scheduled to leave. Finally three more men came through the door and I knew instantly that these were military men not security officers. "Get up" the officer said, in broken English. "You must come with us at once." "Where are you taking me?" I began to ask but was told to shut up and do as I was told. One of the officers came behind me and to my shock, pulled my arms back and handcuffed me. I started to say something and the officer once again told me to shut up and not to say anything else.

I was pushed out of the room, through a door and into an underground parking lot. They continued pushing me towards a van which was open and I was pushed inside. I fell headfirst into the van which had no seats except for the driver and passenger. It was painful as I landed on my shoulder, but not as painful as the handcuffs which were now starting to cut into my wrists.

After a few minutes the van came to a stop and the side door once again opened. Each of the officers grabbed me by the arms and literally dragged me into what seemed to be the back door of a building. Once inside I was taken down a dark hall and we finally stopped in front of what looked like a jail cell. A third guard came over and unlocked the cell and I was pushed inside.

By now I was getting angry and I called out, "what is going on here?" "why are you doing this to me?" They just ignored me and began to walk off. "Can you at least take these hand cuffs off?" I pleaded, but they just turned their backs and walked away. I walked over to a cot at the back of the cell and I laid down my head trying to get as comfortable as I could. After what seemed several hours I fell asleep.

I was awakened several hours later as the cell door opened. Through my blurred vision I saw two men in suits. My arms ached from being behind my back. "Who left the hand cuffs on this man?" the older man asked. "Get them off him right now" he demanded. I was glad to hear an American voice even if I was in a jail cell. Quickly one of the guards came over and took them off. It was like my arms were frozen as I tried to bring them back to my body. "I have to pee so bad my eyes are floating" I said. "Could I have a minute of privacy?" I asked humbly. "We'll be right outside he answered. "just let us know when you are finished." I wasn't sure how long I had been in that cell, but I knew the only thing I had eaten was a muffin and some milk.

"Come with us," said the younger of the two men. "May I ask what is happening to me?" I asked. "You'll know soon enough" he replied as we walked down the hall. A door opened and I was led inside a well lit room with a desk and two chairs. By now I was getting some circulation back in my arms but they still ached badly. "Have a seat" said the older man. "My name is Kramer and this is agent Johnson." Agent Kramer was a big man, no hair and probably in his fifties, on the other hand, was much younger, maybe in his thirties. He had red hair, just over 6' tall and looked very strong. He completely filled out his shirt that was for sure.

"Sorry about the handcuffs" he continued. "They don't do things here like we do back in the States. Would you like some water?" he asked. I nodded my head and then said, "could I get something to eat as well. I haven't had anything to eat in a very long time." He nodded to the guard at the door and said "see what you can find him to eat."

Agent Kramer then said, "I guess you know why you are here." I looked at him and said "I have zero idea of why I'm here or what I have done to be in this situation." "Are you aware of the Embassy bombing yesterday morning?" he asked." Yesterday, I thought to myself. "Had it been that long already." I heard the sirens and then turned on the TV and saw what had happened I said. "That was horrible and I knew that was going to cause a major political stir here, so I quickly packed and headed for the airport. That's when I was grabbed and the police brought me here."

"Let's cut to the chase Mr. Chambers," agent Johnson said. "We have reason to believe that you had something to do with that bombing." I couldn't believe what I was hearing. "Tell us your story" he continued.

I told them where I was from and that I had come here as an aide to my boss, Mr. Zahari. I explained where I had stayed and what I did in the few hours I was in Dubai. I also gave them my whole life history including who I worked for, where I went to university, and information about my family.

"Did you know what was in the briefcase that you delivered?" he asked. "Yes I opened it and there was a flask and an envelope, but I never opened either" I said. "Is this the brief case?" he asked pulling one up from behind the desk. "No," I replied. "That one is my own personal case but the other one was almost exactly the same." "Would you give us the combination?" Kramer asked. "84664" I replied" would you like me to open it for you?" I asked. No thanks, We can do that he answered handing it off to the guard. The guard tried for a couple of minutes to open the case but couldn't do it. "What was the combination again?" Johnson asked. It's" 84664" I said again as he once again tried to open the lid. "Are you sure you don't want me to help with that?" I asked. "Ok" said Kramer handing the case to me while at the same time pulling a gun from his back holster and stepping back a bit.

I put the numbers in order and tried to open the case but it wouldn't budge. I tried again and still the same results. "Is it possible that you confused that combination with another one?" Kramer asked. My head was still buzzing from the lack of food and the aching of my body. I was very confused as I tried to think of another combination but my mind was blank.

"We did find a similar number in your wallet with the same number of letters" Johnson said. Let's see, he continued. "It looks like 61854" he said as he held the paper up with a piece of tweezers. Then it hit me. Is it possible that during my time asleep or while I was at the airport could someone have traded me cases? I knew for a fact that I had never written down that combination anywhere so how did it get in my wallet.

Once again the guard took the case and applied the other combination. He gently lifted the case very slowly and gently as if there could be an explosive inside. It took several minutes before he finally lifted the lid exposing the flask and the letter. Things were starting to make sense and I started to believe this was a set up and I was being framed. "Is this you case?" Kramer asked me again. "No" I replied "this is the one I delivered to the café" I said. "I have no idea how it got back in my possession." Agent Johnson was wearing latex gloves and never took out the items inside.

"Agent Johnson, take this to the lab and have it analyzed" Kramer said. "Oh and check for finger prints as well" he continued. My heart sunk when Kramer said that because I knew my prints were all over that case. We have been analyzing your story for several hours now and will have more conclusive information on you in a few hours.

Guard, take Mr. Chambers back to his cell and we will meet with him later this afternoon. As I walked back to the cell another guard arrived with some food. It was a small half sandwich and a bowl of soup. Once inside I gobbled it down. Normally I'm sure it wouldn't have been very special but for now it was as good as if I were eating a piece of prime rib!

After eating my food I sat and tried to figure out what was happening. How could they possibly think I had anything to do with a bombing? My friends always considered me the peacemaker, the guy who was never in trouble, and the guy who willingly helped everyone. If I was part of a plot I would be the last guy to choose. Granted, I had always been an avid hunter and owned a few guns. I had boxed when I was younger and I knew how to take care of myself but hardly enough to be confused with James Bond. I thought again and finally concluded they had mistaken me for someone else. I have good credentials, a good job and reason for being in Dubai and a boss who could bail me out, that is if they could find him.

It was several hours later that Kramer and Johnson returned. They took me back to the same room where I had been interviewed before. I noticed the mirror on the wall in front of me and assumed it was one way glass.

"Mr. Chambers, both agent Johnson and myself work for the United States CIA" he said. "I want you to know that you are in a great deal of trouble. There is a lot of evidence against you and we will go over it with you. Hopefully you will cooperate fully and we can get some questions answered." "I have nothing to hide" I relied." Ok then let's get down to business."

"We have been looking at your comments from this morning and we have a number of problems with them."

1. You told us you were hired as a worker with a law firm in New York called Foreman, Hudson and Zakari? "is that true," Kramer asked. "Yes that's true" I replied. "Well our agents back home cannot find a law firm named that anywhere in New York." "Not only that, but the building you told us you worked at is vacant and the landlord said it hasn't been rented for over a year." That's

not possible, I was just there two days ago" I exclaimed. "So you are sticking to your story, Mr. Chambers? "Yes" I replied." Note that Johnson," he continued as the agent made notes on his laptop.

2. "You told us you came here as an aide to a Mr. Zakari from your firm." Yes, "I said again." Once again, we have no information on Mr. Zakari." The airlines have no record of him being on the plane. The hotel has not had anyone registered by that name and we don't even have someone with that name in our entire CIA files. How do you explain that?" Kramer asked. "I can't explain it but please believe me I'm telling you the truth."

3. "You told us that you received an expense card from your boss after he paid for your room at the hotel." "Yes that's true" I said. "How often did you use that card?" Kramer continued. "I used it only twice" I said, "once for food brought to my room and once for the cab driver who took me to the café'." "It shows here that you have been using this card for over a week for several different reasons" said Kramer. "It looks like you spent over $10,000 over the past few days." "Just how much do you make a year?" Kramer asked. "It's not even my card" I said, it was given to me. "Then why does it have your name on it?" Chambers he asked. "Are you getting all of this garbage Johnson?" he continued. "Yes Sir" he replied. It was at that point that I realized agent Kramer was getting frustrated. "Should I go on Mr. Chambers or do you want to change your story?" "Honest I am telling you the truth," I replied.

4. "You told us you delivered the package to a café called Europo's," is that true? "Yes Sir," "I could even show you where it is," I answered? I don't think so" replied Kramer, "we went to the spot you told us about and no café exists." Let's go on, he said.

5. "How much money do you have in your account currently?" Kramer asked. I have a couple of thousand in savings and a little less in my checking." Agent Johnson handed him a piece of paper. Kramer held it up to me and asked. "Is this your account?" I looked at it and said "Yes it is." "Then check for me and tell me how much you have in savings" he continued. I was in complete shock! "Uh! It says I have over $250,000 in that account" I stuttered. "And you are telling me you have over a quarter of a million dollars in an account that you don't know about?" Kramer shouted. By now I was going into shock. Was this a bad dream and was I going to wake up or could this really be happening to me?
6. "You told us that you didn't know what was in that briefcase. Do you want to deny that too?" he asked. "I told you what was in it" I replied. "So you are telling me you didn't know what was in the flask?" he continued. "No" I replied, a bit agitated, "I told you I never opened it." "Well both the flask and the envelope have your prints on them," he continued. "Well, we believe that the flask held some sort of detonation device and the envelope has a map of the Embassy."
7. "What kind of wine were you taking back to the U.S.?" Johnson asked me. "I don't know" I answered "but they said it was the boss's favorite." "I have no idea what kind it was", I continued, "I don't even drink." "Well, we almost missed your little message" he said. "We opened the bottle and drained it and at the last second we decided to look under the cap and what do you think we found?" "I have no idea" I said shrugging my shoulders. "I told you I don't drink." "Well we found a number and after tracing it found it was a bank account, in your name." "Let me guess" I said mockingly, another quarter of a million in that one too?" "Well you finally admitted to something." "I never

admitted to anything, I was just being sarcastic" I answered. "Well, if that was a guess you guessed right and this account just happens to be off shore in the Cayman Islands, but I'm sure you didn't know about that either did you Mr. Chambers."

8. "Chambers, is there even one thing you can tell us that is the truth?" Kramer said as his face grew red? "Just give us something, anything, that will help us believe that you had nothing to do with that bombing and the grotesque murder of a least six Arab citizens and a few more locals," he yelled getting louder with each sentence. I just sat in silence. "Just be grateful that the government here turned you over to us. If they hadn't you'd be a dead man by now." They are hopping mad and they want some answers he yelled in my face.

The questions went on for what seemed forever as the two agents continued to interrogate me. Asking the same type of questions over and over, obviously trying to find a crack in my story. "Do you have a good lawyer Mr. Chambers?" Johnson asked. "You better find the best one in your Harvard Law school because I think you are going away for a long, long time." Finally, after several hours of questioning I was escorted back to my cell. I hardly slept at all that night waiting for the morning to come and the next chapter in my life.

As we arrived back in New York by private jet, I was amazed to see several networks waiting outside the gate. It was obvious that my name had been released to the public and I had been found guilty, by everyone in the country. I hadn't been able to talk to anyone during my three day ordeal. I still believed in justice, and even though I was all over TV, newspaper and other news media as the prime suspect in the terrorist bombing in Dubai.

As we left the plane I was handcuffed and taken into a small building and then put into a van and taken to the city jail. I had never wanted to be a criminal lawyer but I did know enough about it to realize that I did have some rights. I was told that I would be held in a private cell until my hearing. I was asked if I wanted to use my phone call to contact a lawyer and I said "Yes." They took off my handcuffs and handed me a cell phone. I knew this would happen and so I decided to phone one of my law professors. I knew he was retired from public duty but he was the one who had mentored me and stood beside me in those years at Harvard.

"Hello Doctor Walker" I said as a voice answered the phone. "Yes this is he" came the answer. "With whom am I speaking?" he asked. Its Phillip Chambers I said. There was a pause on the other end of the line and then the voice came back. "Phillip you seem to be in a great deal of trouble." "To say the least" I replied. I really need your help Sir, I am only allowed one call and I was hoping you could come down and help me with this. "Where are you?" he asked. "I don't know but I can promise you this I had nothing to do with the murder of all those people." "Yes son" he said "I'll get there as soon as I can." "Wait a second and I'll find out where I am." I looked at the officer and he said he would take care of it and give directions to the professor. As he was leaving I asked. "Is there any way I could contact my parents?" "Come on Chambers you are a lawyer you know the rules."

As my jail cell closed I felt the tears welling up in my eyes. "Why did they choose me I thought to myself." Was I the only graduate who jumped at the first job offer that came along? Why didn't I do a little more due diligence before I jumped on board? How did they know about me? What will happen to me now?" These and many more questions raced through my head. I went to the sink and got a drink and then laid down on the bed. I finally fell asleep for the first time in a very long while.

I was startled back to consciousness when I heard someone say, "Chambers, you've got a visitor." I followed the officer to a room with a table and two chairs. I was left there and in a minute Doctor Walker entered the room. He had a British accent and he always reminded me of Sean Connery. He had a white beard and was losing some of his hair on top. I was so happy to see him that I walked over and gave him a hug. Tears started streaming down my cheeks as I pulled away. "Thanks so much for coming," I said. "I've got a lot to tell you." "I don't usually cry like this" I said. "But I've had a very emotional three or four days." "Let's sit down and talk" Doctor Walker said. "Let's see what we can do for you."

For the next couple of hours I explained my story and I tried to tell him everything I could remember. He listened patiently while I retold my eventful trip. Once in a while he would ask a question but mostly it was me just blabbering away.

"Well that's about it" I said. "Phillip, if you are telling me the truth, and I believe you are, we have an enormous amount of work ahead of us. I am going to consult with some of my old partners and see what we can come up with." "Doctor Walker, I know you can't say much to them, but would you drop by and see my parents and tell them there has been a big mistake and that I'm not guilty and that I'm OK?" "Of course I will, and I'll be back to see you tomorrow" he said as he left. "Thanks again" I said as he walked away. The guard then said "OK Chambers let's go back where you belong."

Over the next couple of weeks we began to put forth my case. The evidence we had was simply that I had been framed and had little evidence to show otherwise. Dr. Walker said he put together a group of law school students and a former criminal law partner of his to research my claims. They included going to the building and finding out how the law firm I worked for had disappeared over night. I did not know many people in the firm and those I did know were not good friends, just associates.

I was talking with Dr. Walker and said to him," I know you have gone out on a limb for me in getting all these people on my team. Hey, I laughed for the first time in forever, but at least I should be able to pay, them since I have so much money in the bank. "That would be funny if you really were able to keep the money" Walker said. "The government has either frozen it or taken it away from you." "It really doesn't matter to me it was not mine anyway" I replied. "You know Phillip, I have an idea that may help you." "What's that? I asked. "The money may be very relevant to your case. Why don't you give me your power of attorney and I'll see if I can put both of those accounts in some sort of freeze mode where the government or maybe even those who set you up can't get the money." "That would be fine with me," I answered. "I have a copy in my case" he said, "The government will be steaming mad if you get to that money before they do he laughed." "Is there any way they can trace that money and find out where it came from?" I asked. "We are already working on that angle," Walker replied.

"Well Phillip, let me give it to you straight" he said. "Two weeks of work and we have almost nothing. Dan checked the location of the law firm and nobody is talking. He told me a short time ago that he is sure the office was there but everybody is completely tight lipped. We even had an agent check on that girl Selene that came to your room. We thought that someone as beautiful, as you say she was, would have stood out. The one thing that we did find in Dubai was a store, right where you said it was. It was not a café but instead a wine store. Pretty hard to move a wine cellar" Walker said. But that doesn't help our case because they already know you went there.

"The defense is completely convinced that you were involved in this and no one else is taking credit for the bombing. Usually it is done by some terrorist organization and they want the world to know. In my mind there had to be something in that Embassy that someone wanted badly. Something inside the building that was of great value or information that was top secret. We are getting nothing out of CIA and the way they are keeping a lid on this thing and blaming only you and this stink's like a skunk. Sorry I haven't done more for you son, but you know we'll keep looking," he said as he went to the door and asked for the guard.

I appeared in court the next day for my hearing. I was hand cuffed and shakelled before we left the jail. As we arrived at the court house the outside of the building was jammed with reporters and sign holders. I think it would be safe to say that at that moment I was the most hated man in America. We entered through a well secured door at the back of the court house.

The hearing itself was very short and with no evidence on my behalf, the Judge ordered me held in confinement until he could set a trial date. I thought to myself, how long could that be. Most of these cases take a year to go to court. What was to happen to me I as awaited that court date? It wasn't long before I learned of my fate.

The next morning I was cuffed again and taken into the garage of the Jail. There I was put in a van and taken to a small airport. The ride took a little over an hour and I could tell by the size of the buildings that I was no longer in New York City. I was taken out of the van and then lead down the tarmac to a plane which looked like a commuter jet. I noticed a small sign that said Crandall airport. I had never heard of that place. Once inside I noticed that I was not the only prisoner on board.

There were about twenty others and I was the only white passenger. It seemed to be a mix of different races, some black, some Asian, and some looked Hispanic.

"Where are you taking us?" I asked the guard. "You'll know as soon as you need to" he replied. They then showed me to my seat, did up my seat belt and I heard the engines kick in as we prepared for takeoff. At least two rows separated each of the prisoners and no conversation was allowed.

We were in the air for several hours and the only time we were allowed to move out of our seats was to go to the washroom. A sandwich and a soda were the only things we ate during the entire trip. I was looking out the window and after about an hour, I saw nothing but snow and the frozen tundra for as far as the eye could see. Finally I felt the plane start it's descent and I could hear the wheels being lowered. I looked out the window and caught a glimpse of an air strip and what looked like a large factory.

We circled around and in another few minutes we were sitting on the tarmac. We were each given a blanket as we stepped off the plane and down the stairs leading to the runway. It was bitter cold so I pulled the blanket over my head as well. We walked about one hundred yards until we came to the building I had observed from the air. As we neared the gate I read GREAT NORTHERN PRISON. I thought to myself, "why am I being sent to a prison? I'm just a suspect not a convicted prisoner." The reason would be explained to me to me later that day but for now that is exactly what I was, a Prisoner!

BACK AT GREAT NORTHERN PRISON

To my surprise my name was the first to be called. I did as I was told and headed to the door with a guard trailing behind me. Inside the door was a desk with a middle aged man sitting there. "Hello Mr. Chambers" he said, you are probably wondering why you are here." "As a matter of fact I was "I answered The man speaking to me was a fairly young guy, maybe 30 years old. He opened the door by remote control and said, "Here is your room." I went inside and found it was not like a prison cell at all. It seemed more like a Motel 6 than anything else. The walls were cinder block and except for a single bed a desk and a chair the room was completely bare. There was, however, a sky light and a window in the room, and there was even a bathroom with a shower, sink, and toilet. I set my clothing on the bed and turned to Jones.

"Are all the rooms like this, Mr. Jones?" I asked. "Oh no," he answered. "Not at all, And from now on just call me Tim," he replied. "This is more like a guest room. The others here have actual cells like you have seen in other prisons. Oh, I'm sorry, I didn't mean you had been in other jails, I just thought that you, being a lawyer, had at least seen some." I was a bit surprised to find that he knew I was a lawyer. "Actually I've seen quite a few jails in the past few weeks," I said. "Prior to that I had only seen a couple and that was to talk to friends of mine. I am not a criminal lawyer."

"You've been assigned to me during your stay here," Tim said. "My job is to supervise the facilities here—the pool, the gymnasium, the library, and anything else that the prisoners use. I'm the guy and most of all I'm in charge of security. I checked your record, and after seeing you have hardly ever done anything wrong in your life, I asked the warden if I could use you in the library as a helper," he continued. "I know you have spent a lot of time in libraries over the last few years so you seemed to be the perfect pick for me."

"Hey, I'd really like to do that," I answered. "What is the library like?" I asked. "Well it's not like a normal library you've been in, but it does have books on different trades, teaching techniques, psychology, and things that are there to help the best prisoners learn something while they are here." Tim went on to say that, "Only a few of the prisoners would be allowed to enter the library. First of all a prisoner would have to earn an additional 100 points which would obviously take three months of perfect behavior. Once he has reached that, he would have access to the library for a few hours each day. Right now there are just a handful of men who have access to the library."

"I'm glad you have agreed to work here and while you are there it will be your job to keep things in order and it will give you time to study whatever you like. There are computers in the library as well, with limited internet access. The computers are very well controlled with little access to the outside world with no porn and no games. No e-mail services are available to the prisoners except in special instances. Every e-mail is monitored before it can be sent. That applies to you as well," he continued. "So this prison has good facilities for those who want to get better but it offers nothing in the way of luxury if you can't keep the rules," Tim continued. "The biggest difference between this prison and any other in the world is that there is zero access to the media up here. No way to get here, no way to monitor our activity, and no communication for our inmates," Tim concluded.

With that Tim said, "I'll let you get settled in," and walked out the door. "I'll see you tomorrow and we can start some training for your work in the library." It didn't take me long to learn that even though I was treated with special care because of my situation, I still had to eat and associate with some of the most vicious and radical criminals in the world. On my first day in the cafeteria I could immediately see the various groups sit and talk together. There were so many different languages and cultures in one place.

I sat with, and got to know a few of the guys in the group that first day, and even though many of them were hardened criminals, they were also human beings and many had families and had suffered through some dire circumstances. Although I ate with them and played basketball against them, I really lived in a different world than they did. Many asked why I was there and I explained that I had been charged with murder and that my case was still pending. Strangely enough no one recognized me as the terrorist in the Dubai bombing, so I was left pretty well alone.

I was getting to know my job in the library as time went on. It wasn't the kind of library that you see in small town America. It was quite up to date as far as electronics go, but it didn't have much in the way of reading material except for novels and text books. Every day I learned more about the library and about the men who had access to it.

One day I asked Tim if I could contact any of my family by phone or e-mail. "No phones," he said, but I would be allowed to talk to my parents through the internet. Tim arranged for me to use the e-mail service the next day. I wondered what to tell them and wondered how they would take the news of where I was and what I was doing. Other than having Dr. Walker talk to them, I had been given no opportunity to do so. I knew that my written conversation and communication would be edited, so I carefully wrote out what I wanted to say to them. I looked forward to talking to them even if was just over the internet.

The day before my chat with my parents, Tim invited me into his office. "I have some bad news for you Phil." By now we were on a first name basis. "I just got a memo from New York, telling me that you had been found guilty of all charges." I said, "what? I haven't even been to trial yet." "Why didn't you tell me you had signed a confession?" Tim asked me. "I didn't," I answered. "The e-mail said you had, and when it was presented to the court the Judge found you guilty on all counts." "There's got to be a mistake," I said. "I've had enough of the law profession to know you can't have a trial without the defendant being there." "I guess you can if they've got a signed confession," Tim said.

"Can I call my attorney?" I asked. "It was your attorney who said you gave him the confession." "Does it say what his name was?" I asked. "All I know is the lawyer's name is Walker." I was stunned when I heard his name. Things began to race through my head one after another. Was Walker in on the entire plot from the beginning? Did he take the money out of my accounts, and keep it for himself and then tell the court that I had confessed? Did he use my signature from the release paper I signed? Was he the one who got me the job with Mr. Z in the first place?

"I'm real sorry about this," Tim said. "But there is nothing I can do about it. As soon as the warden gets confirmation of the sentencing I will have to send you to the cells with the other prisoners." "How long does it usually take for that to happen?" I asked. "Oh, probably a month," Tim replied. "But until then I'm going to have you stay right where you are." "Tim, I promise you I had nothing to do with that bombing, but now I'll never be able to prove it." "Strange as it may seem Phil, I really do believe you. Did you still want to speak with your parents?" he asked. "No. I'm sure they are broken-hearted with what has happened. Talking to me will just make them more upset. I know they believe in me and no matter what anyone tells them, they know I would never hurt anyone, let alone kill someone." I turned and left his office and the library and headed directly to my room.

There was only one thought in my mind and that was to escape from this place and prove myself innocent. There was only one way out and that was on the plane that arrived with prisoners and provisions every couple of days. Somehow, some way, I had to get on that plane and back to New York, but that would be my only chance.

I walked to the mirror and looked at myself. I hadn't shaved since I had arrived and thought, "Maybe I do look like a hardened criminal. Well if I ever do escape from here every FBI agent and law enforcement officer will know my face. In that case I better keep the beard and grow my hair as long as I can. I've never had long hair or facial hair in my life so maybe this would be a good cover," I thought.

I spent the next few days trying to think of how I could get on that plane. I began to save a little food each time I ate, knowing that I would have nothing when I arrived back in the city. I watched as each plane came and left. I could see the landing strip from the library. I couldn't help but notice that there were several guards on the plane and I knew that they went to the cafeteria for something to eat as soon as the prisoners were checked in. I also noticed that the food and provisions came in large crates. They were unloaded by a fork lift and taken to the back door of the kitchen. I thought if I could get into one of those crates without being detected I might be able to get out of here.

I needed two things to help me escape. The first was for no one to notice I was gone until the plane had landed some four hours later. I also needed someone to pick me up at the airport and find me a place to hide out. There was only one person that I trusted right now and that was my best friend, Randy. He grew up just down the street from me and he was just like one of the family. He was also my roommate for two years at University before transferring across the country to Stanford, where he became a computer whiz, and now had an office back in New York with Google. I put my plan in motion, hoping the sentence would not be handed down and sent to the prison before I could get out of here.

When we were just kids we always pretended to be spies and we had a code that no one but us understood. Was it simple enough that the technology of today would not be able to figure it out?

I asked Tim about sending that e-mail to my parents and he said I would be allowed to do it. I said to him, "Tim, I would like to send the e-mail to my best friend Randy Troast. He grew up in my house and he's like one of the family. I would like to send it to him and have him deliver it directly to them in person. That way he could tell my story to them and comfort them as well." He said he thought that would be OK and agreed it might be better for my parents if someone were there to comfort them.

"Is it OK to tell my side of the story to them?" I asked. "Sure," said Tim. "That won't be a problem." "Then I'll write the e-mail, give it to you, who then in turn can take it to the security guys for analysis," I said. "Sure, work on it. Bring me a copy and we'll see what we can do for you," he answered.

PLANNING THE ESCAPE

Here was my letter and included in it was our secret code, which simply was to take the second word of each sentence and put together a sentence from the words.

Dear RANDY, I need you to do me a huge favor. I WILL try to be brief and yet to the point. All YOU have to do is tell my parents what has happened to me and comfort them after you read this e-mail to them. Please PICK the best of the points in the story and make them understand that I am innocent. For ME it has been excruciating, thinking about all they have heard about me. I'm UP mentally, considering what has happened to me so far and the fact that I'm probably never getting out of this place. I'm AT my wits end, thinking I will probably never see them again. My CRANDALL family will be devastated as well as all the Chamber family, and probably most of the relatives already are. The AIRPORT runway outside my window will be a constant reminder to me that I will never see the USA again. On SUNDAY a new group of prisoners arrive and at that point I may be sent back to the regular cells. It's NIGHT up here and the days are very short and it can be very depressing. I have been allowed to work in the library for the time I have been here. I have been treated very well and even have my own room. You have always been my best friend and I love you like a brother. Thanks for doing this for me.

But here is my entire story and I swear to you it's all true. It all started . . . .

When I finished the entire letter I took a copy to Tim who then took it to the warden hoping that it would be approved and that Randy would pick up on the code. That was the easy part, getting on that plane would be much tougher. The way I looked at it was simple. Either I take a chance on escaping or spend the rest of my life in prison.

The next morning Tim informed me that he had received permission for me to send Randy my e-mail. "Nothing was deleted," he continued. "So I hope it does for you and your family what you intended it to do. I read it and it sounds very convincing to me. Getting to know you have convinced me that you are innocent," Tim said. "I work for one month up here at a time and then I get one month off. If there is anything I can do to help you while I'm back in New York I would be happy to do so." "Thanks," I said. "I don't think there is anything that anyone can do. By the way, where do you live in New York?" I asked. "Oh I have a little studio apartment near central park," he said. "Isn't that really expensive?" I asked. "Yes, but it's worth it because I live alone, so it's nice to have so many restaurants close by." "What is the name of your apartment complex?" I asked. "My office was just a few blocks from there," I continued. "Dunbar," he answered. "Have you heard of it?" he asked. "No, can't say I have, but I'm sure it's nice," I replied. "When do you go back?" I asked. "I just got here a couple of weeks before you did. I won't be back in New York for quite a while. By the way, I would just appreciate it if you would be my friend while you are stuck in here. I'll do what I can to make your stay comfortable," Tim said. "Even after they move you will still be allowed to visit the library a couple of hours a day." "I'm sure that will be the best part of each day," I laughed.

I had to get a lot done in the next week, if I were able to make this happen. One thing that was in my favor is that a number of the employees of the prison used the library on a regular basis and I had been able to get to know them on a first name basis. Joel was the head chef and he often had me come in the kitchen to taste some of his new recipes just before it was time to eat. I decided to make a surprise visit to the kitchen that day.

"Hi Joel, I said. "Do you have anything new and interesting to eat today? I'm starving and was wondering what was on the menu," I continued. "Not really," he replied. "Chicken fried steak with all the trimmings. Does that sound good to you?" he asked. "Sounds great to me," I replied. "By the way, how do you determine what to make each day?" I asked. "Do you pre-order stuff like once a week or once a month?" I continued. "Actually our stuff is pretty fresh," he said. "We get food flown in every few days," he answered. "You see these containers?" he said pointing at the wall by the door. I looked at them and they were about four feet by four feet wooden crates. I thought to myself, "Could I fit in there and stay there for several hours?" I noticed the crates had been closed and I noted how they had been sealed. I knew that I would need some sort of tool to close the box on myself once I was inside. "How do they keep the food refrigerated, especially the meat?" I asked. "They send some of it frozen," he answered. It's real cold in the cargo bay of the plane, so it's still fine when it arrives here. We just put it straight into the fridge and freezers once the food arrives." "What about Ice cream?" I asked trying not to indicate what I was up to. "Like I said, the cargo is cold enough to keep it mostly frozen and sometimes they pack it in dry ice," he answered. "Well, I'm ready for that chicken fried steak," I said.

"Let's eat." I walked out the door with a greater understanding of what I had to do.

After dinner I went back to the library and did some work. Tim came in as I was sorting some of the books. "Hi Tim," I said. "Any news on when I can send my e-mail?" I asked. "I think it's already gone," he answered. "I'll let you know if and when you get a reply." "Thanks," I said. "I'm looking forward to it."

Tim had no worries about me, and left me in charge when he was checking his other areas or went to dinner. I was not allowed to go into his office on my own but I noticed that he seldom locked the door when he went out. I knew he had a closet in his office and I was hoping maybe I could find something in there that would keep me warm on the flight. If he has a winter jacket in there he would probably not use it until it was time for him to return home.

When he left to check on the gym, I snuck inside and opened the closet. Sure enough, there was a jacket and a winter coat. I saw a suit hanging there, as well and a shirt. I quickly closed the door and left his office just as a couple of the prisoners entered the library.

During the next couple of days I spent a little more time in the kitchen with Joel. I asked him if he would show me how to prepare some of his dishes. By doing that I was able to see, first hand, the delivery of the food when it arrived from the plane on the fork lift. I was lucky enough to see two deliveries and I also saw when the crew came back and took the crates back to the plane. I noticed that after the boxes were emptied that the kitchen staff closed them back up. The crates had a simple clasp system and I wondered how, after I got in I would be able to seal it closed again.

I figured that if I had a hammer and a screwdriver inside I could put a screw into the wood panel and pull it toward me with the hammer. Hopefully that would pull it far enough in to make the clasp secure itself. There were a lot of if's involved in my escape. One little slip up and I knew I was toast.

Tomorrow was Sunday. I had to be ready and must have everything in place. I couldn't sleep at all that night trying to make sure I had figured out everything correctly. Sunday morning couldn't come fast enough for me. I had to work fast and methodically if I wanted this to work.

During the night I wrote a letter which I addressed to Tim. It said:

Tim I have been thinking about what has happened to me over the past few weeks and I've come to a conclusion. The fact is I can't stay here in prison for the rest of my life, knowing I did nothing wrong. I have decided to leave and see what happens. I know there is nothing out there but I would rather die in the wilderness than rot in here. I'm story but I stole your winter jacket and hat. You have been a great friend to me and I appreciate all you have done for me. Hope life is good to you, I left the note on the table, hoping that it would buy me some time if they found out I was gone. I needed to at least arrive in New York before they figured out that I possibly escaped on the plane.

I went to the library around noon. I said, "Tim, I'm not feeling very well today. I think I must have some kind of flu." "Well, don't give it to me," he replied. "I've always found that the best way for me to get rid of something like this is to sleep it off," I continued. "I hardly slept at all last night and I'm so tired. It would really help if I had a sleeping pill. Tim. Do you have any or is it against the rules?" I asked. "I have some in my room," he answered. "I'll go get you one. I don't think you can OD on just one," he laughed. "I appreciate that," I said. "I'll be right back," he said as he headed out of the library and down the hall.

The second he left the room I headed for his office, I opened the closet and took out his winter jacket and toque. I quickly headed right back to my room, opened the door and put them inside. I then returned to the library. Tim returned in a minute with a sleeping pill for me.

"Are these very strong?" I asked. "They put me out for a good eight hours," replied Tim. "Ok," I said. "I'm headed back to bed and I probably won't see you again until tomorrow. Thanks for everything Tim." "No problem, Phil. I hope you sleep well."

THE ESCAPE

With that I left the library and headed back to my room. I rolled the sheets up and covered them with a blanket, so it looked like someone was still in my bed. I then tucked the pillow under the blanket and said to myself, "Hey, that looks pretty good." I knew the plane was to arrive shortly. I waited and when I heard it land I checked the hall, grabbed Tim's Jacket and headed for the Kitchen.

As I entered the kitchen Joel said, "Hey, what's with the jacket?" "I wasn't feeling too good, so Tim let me borrow his jacket and I went outside to get some fresh air. I'm tired of being cooped up in that library so I thought I'd come down and help you guys in here. Is that OK?" I asked. Just then the service door opened and the fork-lift made its way into the storage area. "What did you get this week?" I asked Joel. "Never really know what I'm going to get until it gets here and I open up the crates," he replied. "Do you need some help unloading?" I asked. "Sure. Come on, let's see what surprises we got today." I walked with Joel back where the crates were and threw my jacked back in the corner.

For the next half an hour we unloaded the two crates. I helped the kitchen crew unload all the food from the boxes and hauled them to their designated areas. I watched intently as one of the men grabbed a small crow bar and pulled open the crate. Once he opened the crate he returned the crow bar to the tool box. I thought to myself that the crow bar would be even better than a hammer to help with my escape. Once we had unloaded all of the boxes the workers pushed the lid of the crate back onto the clips.

I knew getting into the crate would be tricky. There were three other workers in the kitchen besides Joel. I realized that the fork lift and its operator would be back shortly to pick up the empty crates. I continued to stand by Joel, pretending to admire his work. "Do you want to help set up the buffet table?" Joel asked. "No, I'd better get going," I said as they prepared to move some items through the kitchen doors and into the cafeteria. "I'll just grab my jacket," I said. "I think I left it back in the warehouse." "Ok," said Joel. "I'll see you later today then."

I only had a minute to make this work. I headed straight for the tool box, grabbed a long nail and the crow bar and headed for the crate. I hoped the workers would not hear the noise. Just as I was to pull open the crate, I heard one of the workers come back to the kitchen and head toward the back. I hid behind the crate as he came nearer and nearer to me. I found it amazing that he didn't see me because he walked right past me. I held my breath as he turned the other way and headed back toward the kitchen. As soon as he was out of sight I grabbed the crow bar and pried open the case. There was a pop as the crate separated from the clips that held it firm. I quickly climbed inside and pulled the lid back toward me. Fumbling in the dark, I placed the nail on the side of the lid and then, using the crow bar as a hammer, began to drive the nail into the wood.

I would pound for a minute and then listen to see if I could hear anyone in the kitchen. I continued to do this until I felt the nail was secure. I listened once more and heard no sound so I pulled the nail toward me with the claw of the bar and to my delight heard the clips click together and the crate was sealed.

I sat down in my little enclosure satisfied with how it had gone but at the same time petrified that I would still be caught and spend the next month in solitary confinement. During the next hour or so I tried to make myself as comfortable as I could in this four foot by four foot space. I was sure this would be the easiest part of the trip.

It seemed forever before I heard the garage door open and the sound of the fork lift filling the room. I waited as the lift pushed its forks through the pallets and lifted the crate in the air. I could tell that the lift had left the building just by the instant drop in temperature. I could feel it as it left the hard ground and went up onto the tarmac. The next thing I felt was the fork lift going up an incline and into the cargo portion of the plane. And then as fast as it happened, I heard the door shut and I was alone for what was going to be a cold and long trip back to New York.

I was part way there and thought about many things, the most important being if Randy had received my e-mail and deciphered the code. If he hadn't, I would be a sitting duck walking down the road in an orange prison jump suit. I felt the plane's engines start up, then it turned and taxied down the run way. It went to the end of the runway, turned again and headed for takeoff. In a matter of a minute I was in the air and on my way back to New York. In just a half hour after we left I began to feel the cold coming into the crate. Joel was right. Nothing would ever thaw out at this altitude. I pulled the toque all the way over my head and tried to pull my legs up under the jacket to try and stay warm. I was already glad I had put on three pair of socks this morning.

I knew that I was alone in the cargo hold and as cold as I was getting, I thought maybe I should climb out of the box for a while. Still, something inside me said that if I did and got caught my life would be over. I don't think I have ever been that cold for so long. As the hours passed I could hear the steady hum of the engines echoing in my head. Finally I dozed off and fell into a deep sleep. I hadn't had any sleep for a long time. When I awoke I felt like every muscle in my body would break. I had been in the same position for at least a couple of hours. The good thing was that I could feel us descending and that gave me some hope that this ordeal would be over one way or another in a few more minutes.

I knew that it would be after dark when we arrived, and wondered if the crates would be moved again before the plane was put away for the night. It seemed we taxied along the tarmac for a long time before we finally stopped. I had to get out of that box before I went crazy but once again my instinct told me to sit still for a while longer. Sure enough I heard someone open the door to the cargo hold. "Do you want to move and unload this stuff or wait until morning?" I heard one man say. "Tomorrow will be good enough," replied the other person in the plane. "Ok, then let's get out of here," said the first voice. I heard them leave and then I let out a sigh of relief. I waited a few more minutes and the grabbed the crow bar and pushed it against the crate. It didn't budge so I pushed harder and still nothing. I thought to myself, "Had the steel latches frozen up during the flight?" I then pushed my legs up against the lid and pushed again, but my legs were so cramped, I couldn't get any leverage. "All this way and I can't even get out of this stupid box," I thought to myself. By now I was getting desperate. Once again I pulled my knees back and pushed forward with all my might. The lid didn't open but I did hear it crack. I tried it again and the lid loosened and fell away from the crate.

I crawled out of my private freezer and into the cargo hold. I could barely move my legs, so I just rolled onto the floor. It took a few minutes for my body, especially my legs to recover. I stood up and pushed the lid back on the crate. I then hobbled to the front of the hold. I grabbed the door, hoping it would open and that I wouldn't spend the rest of the night in the plane. I was sure everyone was gone, but I turned the handle slowly. To my pure pleasure the handle turned and opened up. I saw a ladder which, I was sure, went up into the cabin. I climbed up and pushed open the hatch and came up in the area that the flight attendants would normally occupy. I was finally loosening up, and pulled myself into the body of the plane.

I noticed that the plane was still outside next to a building. It was dark, but I recognized it as the place we had boarded the plane only a few weeks earlier. I walked to the front of the plane and looked out the window. It was dark outside but I could still see some activity near the runways outside. I couldn't see anyone on the side of the plane that provided my exit, so I pushed open the door. I was pleased to see the ladder to disembark was still there. I climbed down the stairs and headed for the edge of the building looking for some cover. I knew I needed to get rid of the crow-bar so I dumped it in a garbage dumpster as I made my way toward the entrance of the airport.

When I reached the far end of the building, I looked around the corner and I could see the entrance about two hundred yards away. I knew there were people in the area and even saw a couple walk through the parking lot that separated me from the entrance. I watched them get in their cars and drive to the toll booth where they paid the attendant and then drove off. I knew I had to get out by going past the toll booth. Everywhere else the fence was high and had barbed wire on the top. I had no choice but to either sneak past the attendant or walk right by him.

The other problem I had was where would Randy be waiting for me? I couldn't have given him any more information on the e-mail so he just had to be by that front gate. I made my way through the parking lot undetected and then came the moment of truth. I was only thirty feet from the booth when I began walking towards the street. My orange jumpsuit would normally have given me away but I assumed that many who worked at the airport would wear orange as well.

I got up my courage and walked right toward the booth. Just as I was about to walk past the worker inside, I heard a voice say, "Hey!, Where are you going, kid?" I turned and looked at him and said, "Hey man, I just finished my shift and was going home but I've lost my keys. "Do you want me to call a wrecker?" he asked. "It's a long walk back to town." "I called one of my buddies, and he's going to meet me here at the gate," I said. "By the way, which car is yours?" he asked. "It's the 2000 Chevy pickup near the end of the lot." I answered. "Well, let me see your security pass," he said, "or I'm going to have to make you wait until security comes out and clears you."

I knew this was do or die for me. Tthe thought came to me that it was time to start running. Then I heard another voice. It said, "Hey man are you coming or not?" I looked up and saw the long lost face of my buddy Randy. I then turned to the attendant and said, That's my ride man! Do still want me to wait for security?" I asked. Randy standing there must have given me some credibility and so he said, "No, get going and have a nice night." "See you tomorrow," I said to the attendant as I walked toward Randy's waiting vehicle. I got in and we pulled away from the airport and on to the main highway.

BACK IN NEW YORK

I looked over at Randy and said, "I love you man. You just saved my life." "What in the heck is going on with you, Philly?" he had always called me that growing up. "This is the craziest thing I've ever done in my life." "You think your life is crazy?" I questioned him. "You have no idea what crazy is. All I know is that you remembered the code and you came to get me. I'll tell you the whole story when we get somewhere safe. Hey, there's a Wendy's," I said. "I haven't eaten anything since yesterday. Go through the drive through and get me the biggest burger they've got. I've got to go to the bathroom," I continued. "I've been holding it for hours." "By the way, I almost didn't recognize you," Randy said. Let's get to my apartment." "I can't stay there." I replied. "Once they find out I've escaped and know I'm not dead in that northern wilderness, they will come looking for you." "Yes, but where will you stay?" Randy asked. I reached into my pocket and pulled out a set of keys. "See this one," I said, pulling it apart from the other two. "Yes. What does it say on there?" he asked, seeing it was engraved on. "It says Dunbar," I replied. "Take me to down-town New York and let's find an apartment complex with that name."

"Who owns this place?" Randy asked. "Actually it belongs to a guy named Tim who I worked for in the prison. In fact he is head of security for the prison I was in, which is the newest and most modern in the world," I continued. This guy is a former FBI and CIA agent and at the very top of the charts. "Does he know you are going to stay in his condo?" Randy asked. "Not a chance," I answered. "But I found these keys in his coat when I borrowed it. He isn't back in New York for a couple of weeks and I couldn't find a better place to hide than right under the nose of one of the prison's main guys," I laughed. "Before we go there, I need you to stop at Walmart and get me some dye for my hair and beard. I think it's finally time for a change," I chuckled.

Randy and I walked up to the apartment building. It was just past midnight and I hoped the key would give me access to the three story structure. I looked at the directory and there it was. Tim Cushing was his name and I was glad there was only one Tim in the directory. Sure enough, the key fit and we were inside. Number 203, It said on the key as I took to the stairs, followed closely by Randy. "Here it is," said Randy as he got to the top of the stairs. "I hope he doesn't have a security system inside his condo," I said. "Or we are hooped. I slid the key and entered the apartment.

Tim's studio apartment was very nice indeed and a perfect spot to operate from. Tomorrow I would begin my investigation. I'm sure my name would be front page news as soon they found out I had escaped. Fortunately for me, after I dyed my hair I wouldn't look anything like Phillip Chambers. Randy and I talked and realized that we could have almost no contact for the next few weeks. He was the only person I had contacted while I was in prison and would be their only lead. The only place that would be safe to meet would be Tim's apartment and that was if Randy knew he wasn't being followed.

I fell asleep on the bed and he slept on the couch. Randy had to be at work in the morning so we only had a few minutes to talk. If anyone could find the people who had framed me, it was Randy. Working for Google he would be able to track what had happened to me as well as research the backgrounds of anyone involved in my case. I gave him a list of the people involved and he vowed to go to work on his new pet project of proving me innocent.

I went to the bathroom, dyed my hair and showered. It was a medium brown color and as I looked in the mirror even I didn't recognize myself. I trimmed my hair until I had a goatee and mustache with sideburns all the way down. I then put on the sun glasses I bought at the store and I knew the disguise was complete. I then got dressed and headed out to get something to eat for breakfast. Randy bought me a couple of shirts and pants, and gave me five hundred dollars in cash. He also gave me a bank card to buy some new clothes. He brought me a gun and a couple of extra clips. I hoped I would never have to use it, but I had shot many times at the shooting range and at least knew how to handle one.

I went downstairs, turned left at the bottom of the building and headed down the side walk. I noticed a little coffee shop just down the road and across the street. I walked inside and ordered a breakfast sandwich and a glass of orange juice. After breakfast I walked down toward my office, or at least where my office once was. Sure enough, there was nothing but a vacancy sign on the door with a number to call if someone was interested in renting the building. I wrote down the number and headed for my new home.

When I arrived home I called the number on the sign and a woman answered the phone. "This is John Clayton calling and I was wondering if I could get some information on the building you have for rent down on 7th Avenue." "Let me turn you over to Lisa," she answered. She is in charge of our commercial department." I waited a few moments and Lisa answered the phone. "Hello Mr. Clayton. I understand that you are interested in our property over on 7th." "Yes, that's correct," I said. "I was wondering if I could arrange for a viewing." "Sure," she said. "What line of work are you in, Mr. Clayton?" she asked. "I am the operations manager for a marketing company," I answered. "We are a fairly new company and need to form a call center. Do you know if your building is wired well enough to handle that?" I asked. "I'm sure it would," she answered. "When would you like to meet and tour the facility?" she asked. "I just rented an apartment near that building, and I have one other viewing this afternoon at two. I should be done by three, so how would four o'clock be?" "That would be fine," said Lisa. "I will meet you there if that's OK," she responded. "That would be fine," I replied. "What will you be wearing?" "A red jacket," she said. "So I'll see you at four then." "I'm looking forward to it," I said. "We'll see you then."

I turned on the big screen TV and clicked onto the news. So far there was not a word about me. I had seen a nice little corner store just down the street during my walk and knew I needed some groceries. I had a couple of hours to kill so I headed outside once again. I loaded up with some things to eat and some toiletries and returned to the studio.

COLLECTING THE FACTS

By then it was just past 3:30 and it was time for me to go. I walked toward the building, which was only a ten minute walk from the apartment. I stood across the street watching for Lisa to arrive. A car pulled up and a tall blonde woman got out and headed toward the building. She was wearing a red coat so it had to be her. I watched to see if anything else mysterious was happening and then headed across the street.

"Hi, you must be Lisa," I said as I approached her. "Yes, and you must be Mr. Clayton," she responded, extending her hand. "Just call me John," I said as I shook her hand. She was very attractive and reminded me of Nicole Kidman. I asked her if anyone else ever said that, and she said it had happened several times. I also noticed that she was not wearing a wedding ring. I followed her inside the building and she unlocked the door and walked inside. I could see where the decal had been removed from the glass on the door. There it was, just as I remembered it from a few weeks previous. Everything had been removed and the building had been cleaned and vacuumed.

"How many square feet is this building?" I asked. "It's about 2,000 she replied and another 1,000 in the back that is used for storage." I noticed that there is no one renting the bay across the hall as well. "No," she said. "Both bays have been empty for some time." "What kind of a business was in here last?" I asked. "I'm not sure," she said. "It wasn't one of my accounts. It looks like there were a few phone lines here and looking at the outlets they serviced a few computers." She was quite vague and I could tell she was a bit uncomfortable. "Do you know the software company who serviced this building?" I asked. "I'm not sure," she said. "But I'm sure there are lots of companies that could do that for you." "Do I need to pay for my own utilities or is that part of the lease?" I continued. "In the past we paid the utilities on the building," she answered. "I might be interested in both bays," I said. "Do you have a price for me?" I asked. "Well, if you take both bays the square footage price would certainly be cheaper," she answered. "Well, it looks like something that might interest me. Do you think you could get me a quote?" I asked. "Sure," she said. "Give me your cell number and I'll get right back to you." "I just moved here and I haven't picked up a new phone for this area. My last one was just for a localized area so why don't I call you tomorrow?" "That would be fine. Just call my office tomorrow." Lisa answered.

I looked around for a few minutes and then she showed me the other bay. We then walked back onto the street and when we were about to leave I said, "I'm brand new here and wondered if you knew of a nice place to eat." "There are a quite a few nice ones in the down town area," she replied. "The other question I have is, do you know anyone who looks a lot like Nicole Kidman that would like to go to dinner tonight?" She smiled and inquired, "Are you asking me out?" "I think that is what I'm trying to do," I laughed. "I know you don't know me, but I'm a safe guy and we could just meet somewhere so it wouldn't be uncomfortable for you." She paused a minute and then said, "Normally I would say no, but there is a new Italian garden restaurant just a couple of streets over on 5th avenue and I've been dying to go there." "Then it's a date?" I asked. "Sure," she said. "How about 7:00 o'clock?" she replied. "But it's pretty expensive," she said. "That's fine with me," I said. "I'll look forward to it." I thought to myself, "I wonder how Randy will like seeing this on his debit card?" "Goodbye," she said, and headed for her car. I tried not to watch her walk away because she looked pretty good from all angles, but I quickly turned and headed back across the street.

When I walked back to the apartment I thought to myself, "It sure would be nice to have a set of wheels." That gave me an idea. I had noticed a place to hang keys just inside the door of Tim's apartment. "I'm using his apartment and clothes. Maybe he has a car too," I thought. "If he doesn't leave it at the airport, maybe it's somewhere near here." I walked inside and saw some keys. I looked at them and found a set of GM keys. I grabbed them and headed downstairs to the basement where I assumed there was a parking garage. I was right and headed into the parkade. There were a number of cars, so I headed down the middle of the lot pushing the remote. I had walked halfway down when there was a honk and the lights came on a vehicle parked a few cars down. I was very happy and surprised to see a Cadillac Escalade right before my eyes. I hopped in and sat behind the wheel. I checked the glove compartment and there was Tim's registration. The gas tank was even full. I laughed at the thought of driving this beautiful vehicle, but knew if I ever got stopped by the police I would be finished. "Oh well," I thought. "At least I have some transportation if I get in real trouble."

I got back to the room just in time to hear the buzz from the intercom downstairs. "It's Randy, "came a voice loud and clear from the speaker. "Come on up," I said and buzzed him in. "What has happened today to my criminal friend?" he asked, as he pushed open the door. He then hesitated and stopped, then said, "Wow, I wasn't really sure that was you," he gulped. "Let's see, should I start with the fact that I toured my old office building or that I have a date tonight with a great looking woman?" "Get out of here," he answered. Then hesitating a second said, "You are not serious are you?" "I'm telling you the truth my man," I answered, and then went on to tell him what I had done during the day. I told him about Lisa and how I hoped to get some information out of her at dinner tonight. I also told him that she indicated that she knew nothing about the previous renters in the building, but I could tell by her attitude that I wasn't getting the entire story. "I left the back door in the warehouse section ajar so I can get back in there tomorrow. There was some film on the glass door but some residue is still there. I was hoping you could get me something that would take it off and we could see if any of the names of the law firm is still there." "I think that could be arranged," Randy said. "I'll meet you there for lunch."

"What did you find out today, Randy?" I asked. "I did a little research on your so-called friend, Dr. Walker and he's really well connected. He has a lot of friends in Washington and many are politically strong. I have set up a bit of a data base and I'm trying to put a little puzzle together. I couldn't find anything on your Mr. Zakari, but I've got some pictures of Walker and many of them are with his associates. It's obvious that you were set up by your old professor and those two guys have to be connected somehow. I'll bring them over tomorrow night and we'll see if you can see any familiar faces. I also did a search on your account and according to that you are dead broke. I made sure I did it from a pay phone so they couldn't trace where it came from. By the way, do you know how hard it is to find a pay phone these days? They are almost obsolete," he concluded. "I put a search in on a few of the other people you mentioned and came up with nothing so far, but don't worry I'll keep trying."

"Have you heard anything from the prison or the FBI?" I asked. "I haven't even been home yet but, I'm sure I will," he answered. "But I better get going so you are not late for your hot date," he laughed. "Oh, I forgot to tell you I got you a cell phone," Randy said. "I'm probably the only person in this world you can phone. I figured if you needed me to get you out of another jam you better have some way to contact me." "But is it traceable?" I asked. "Not in the name I used when I purchased them," he replied. "Look," he continued. "I have a matching one. We are now on the family plan," he laughed. "It has a video and camera and you might very well need it if you come along something that you need." "Thank you my dear Watson," I snickered. "No problem Holmes," he said as he closed the door.

I showered and got ready to go to dinner. I had no idea what information I would get from Lisa, but I knew I had to do something. Since I only had two sets of clothing, I thought I would see if any of Tim's things might fit. I was taller and the pants didn't do me any good but the dress shirts fit fine and along with a nice silk tie and a pair of the pants Randy bought me I was ready for dinner. The leather jacket also looked like it was brand new, so I decided to wear it as well.

I went outside and hailed a cab. He pulled over and I got in and said, "There is a new Italian restaurant over on 5th Avenue. Are you familiar with it?" "Yes," he said and pulled out into the light traffic. It was only a short drive and I apologized to him for the short trip but left him a good tip. I walked inside and asked if they had the name Clayton on their reservation list. I had called it in earlier that day. "Yes sir, we do. Wwould you like to be seated?" "Thank you," I said. "That would be fine. Do you have a place that would be fairly private?" I asked giving the host a $20.00 bill. "Oh! Yes sir," he said. "Just follow me and I will seat you now. I noticed you had a reservation for two Mr. Clayton. Will your guest be here soon?" he asked as I slid into the booth. "Actually, there she is now. The beautiful woman in the green dress," I said, pointing to the entrance. "I will get her for you sir," he said politely, and headed toward the desk.

I stood up as she approached the table and took her by the hand and then helped her into the booth. "You look wonderful tonight Lisa," I said. "Thank you," she replied. "You clean up pretty good yourself." "By the way, my first name is John," I said. "Not a tough one to remember." "Ok John," she replied. "I think I can handle that." "I'm glad you came," I said. "I wouldn't have blamed you if you hadn't. You must have not done a background check on me," I laughed. "No, once in a while I just like to trust my instincts and go for it," she answered. "Well, let me tell you a little bit about me and then, if you like what you hear, you can tell me your life's story."

I began by telling her that I had graduated from Harvard and was hired by a marketing firm and had just moved here from the upper part of the state where I was born. Everything else was just a story and so I wasn't sure if I would get the truth from her or not. We talked about her job in real estate and how long she had been with the company. I ended up asking her how long the building I was looking at had been vacant and why. She was a little more receptive this time and said that the company that had it before basically up and left, but paid their lease in full. She did say that it was strange, because they rented both bays, but only used one. "Was it like a business office, or what?" I asked. "I think it was a law firm," she said. "But it wasn't my client," she continued. "My boss took care of that account."

We ordered dinner and talked about everything from families to football. Just before our meal something happened that would forever change my life. I believe things happen for a reason, and if you are an honest good living person, life will give you a break. While Lisa and I were talking a couple walked by our booth, and as the woman brushed by me I could smell the perfume she was wearing. I had only smelled that fragrance once before and it was as intoxicating now as it had been then. I stopped in the middle of a sentence, and Lisa asked," Are you OK?" "Sorry," I said. "I just had a little gas bubble in my throat. Could you excuse me a minute?" I said. "I'll be right back." I stood and headed to the men's room, glancing at the woman who had just entered the restaurant.

MY FIRST BREAK

I couldn't believe my eyes. It was Selene, the woman from Dubai who had been in my hotel room. She looked up at me and I turned my head even though I was sure she wouldn't recognize me. When I returned from the wash room I noticed the man she was with was much older than she was. He looked more like her dad than her date. He had grey sideburns and you could tell by his manner and what he wore that money wasn't a problem. I sat back down across from Lisa and she could tell I was uncomfortable. "Are you alright John?" she asked. "Yes," I answered with a smile. "It was just a little heartburn but I'm good now."

Our meal was delivered and we began to eat. I tried to stay focused, but my mind was playing tricks with me. I knew this was the break I needed to exonerate myself. "But how could I get out of my dinner situation?" I thought to myself. I noticed that the head waiter served the new couple. Obviously the waiter knew the man and was treating him like royalty.

By the time we finished our dinner, Selene and her partner were just getting their meal. "I'm sorry Lisa," I said. "This is very embarrassing, but for some reason my stomach is really bothering me." "I understand," she said. "It happens." "I really need to go home and sleep this off," I continued. "I was hoping to go to a movie or dancing and spend more time with you tonight. Is there a chance you would go out with me again later this week?" I asked. "Of course," she said as we stood to leave.

"Before you go would you mind if I took a picture of you, since I can't take you with me tonight?" "Sure," she said. "That would be fine." I turned her around so she was standing right in front of Selene's table. Instead of just taking her picture I videoed the couple sitting at the table. I could tell they were uncomfortable, as I took a few seconds to snap the shot. I took one last still of Lisa and showed it to her as we walked away. There was a moment when my eyes met Selene's and a small smile graced her lips. I walked Lisa to the door and said, "When will I see you again?" "Whenever you like," she replied. "May I put your number in my cell phone?" I asked. "I got one today, so I won't be completely inaccessible," I laughed. She gave me her number and we walked to the parking lot where her car was waiting. I pulled her toward me and gave her a hug and she kissed me lightly on the cheek. "See you soon," I said as she drove away. I hated to have her leave, but I knew this might be my only chance to see Selene and maybe help unravel the story of my past few weeks.

My dilemma now was did I have time to run home and get the car so I could follow Selene or just wait outside the eatery and follow her with a cab. I decided on the latter. No way could I lose her and who knew how long it would be before they finished eating and left. I returned to the restaurant and slipped inside the door. I walked over to the host and thanked him on the great meal and service and then I asked him, "By the way, who is the gentleman seated in the back corner? He looks so familiar to me." "He is an ambassador to the U.S., but I can't remember what country he is from." "Maybe I've seen him on TV," I laughed. "Once again thanks for everything," I said. "I'll be back". With that I walked out the door and started down the street. I had noticed that the couple had now nearly finished their meal as I left the building.

I grabbed my phone and called Randy. "Hey, where are you right now?" I asked, "And how long will it take to get here?" "I could be therein about half an hour," he answered. "I've run onto something important and I need your help. Jump in your vehicle and get here as soon as you can. I'm going to get a cab and I'll let you know where we are as we go. In the meantime, stay off your cell phone and I'll contact you soon." I hailed a cab and watched as he pulled into the curb. "Where to?" he asked in a very American voice. "I haven't got a clue," I replied, as I looked at the clean cut college aged kid behind the wheel. "I just need you to pull up a bit and wait until I tell you to go. I need to follow someone." "Hey," quipped the driver. "I thought this only happened in the movies." "I hope you are a good driver because no matter what, you can't lose them," I responded.

It was a good fifteen minutes before the couple came out of the door. "That's them," I said. "Let's see where they go.: It didn't take long for a Limo to pull up in front and the two of them got in. The Limo pulled away followed by me in the cab. The driver and I talked as we drove after the limo. "Are you some sort of spy?" he asked. "Or are you just tailing your wife or girlfriend?" "Neither," I said. "Just keep following them." Meanwhile the phone rang and it was Randy, "Where are you?" he asked. "I'm not sure. Here, talk to the cab driver," I said handing him the phone. He gave Randy instructions and he said, "I'm about five minutes behind you. I'll try and catch up."

A few minutes later the Limo pulled up to a Hilton Hotel and Selene was helped out of the car and headed inside. I said to the cabby, "Pull over and wait for me." I handed him my phone and said. "Call my buddy and tell him where you are. Then when he gets here, tell him to park and wait outside and wait for me. He will pay you but I need to go now," I said as I left the cab and headed for the front door.

I knew that she had noticed me at the restaurant and I needed to keep a safe distance away. I waited in the entrance as she approached the desk and then headed for the elevator. I slipped along the wall until I saw the elevator door close. I was glad she was alone in the elevator as it made its way up the shaft. It stopped on the 21st and top floor. At least I knew where she was staying. I returned outside to find Randy sitting in my cab. I opened the door and Randy crawled out. "Here's your phone," said the cabby, holding out his hand toward me. "Thanks," I said. "I appreciate your help tonight." "Hey, I'm Carl and here is my card. That's the most fun I've had since I started this job a few months ago. If I'm ever on when you need a ride, call the center and see if I'm available. By the way are you guys CIA or something? I know," he continued, "that if you tell me, you will have to kill me," he laughed. "Carl, what are you doing here in New York?" I asked. "I'm a down on my luck actor just looking for a break, and I'm really pretty good." "Well, I just might have a job for you," I said. "But for now, you never saw me, right? Remember that," I said as I handed him a crisp $100.00 dollar bill. "Thanks man," he said as he pulled away.

Randy pushed me toward the building and said, "Philly, what's going on? I told him that I had seen Selene and had followed her here to this hotel. "What are the chances of that happening?" he asked me. "That's like winning the lottery," he continued. "I've got some pictures of her and a video as well. I don't know who she is or who she was with tonight but if anyone can find out, it's you." "I don't know if I can," Randy answered. "If this guy is a big wig or involved in some conspiracy and the feds are able to trace this back to me and then to you we'll all go to jail. Can you think of anyone who could do something like that?" I asked. "Not really, but I will work on it."

"I guess there is nothing more we can do tonight, but I'm going to be here early in the morning and find out who she is, and why she is here. But before I came over to the Hotel I was wondering if we could get a print off that door at the old law office," I said. "I brought some stuff that I found on one of our search engines and asked one of the girls at the office to pick it up," Randy said. "Have you got it with you?" I asked. "Right here in the trunk," he replied. "Come stay at the condo with me tonight and we'll give it a whirl the first thing in the morning." I got in the car and we drove back to the condo. "Tomorrow might be a great day," I thought to myself as I got ready for bed. For the first time in forever, it seemed like I finally was getting somewhere.

We got up real early, got dressed and headed to the rental building. We walked around the back and I was happy to see the door was still ajar from the day before. We walked to the front of the office and started to get what was left off the window. It took about fifteen minutes to get the resin and the paper on the window and let it set up. "You think it's ready?" I asked. "That's what the instructions said, Sherlock," Randy laughed. "It wasn't real clear, but there was no doubt we could read Fore, Zak and law. I gave Randy a high five and said, "Let's get out of here." Finally I had my first piece of real evidence. "Where can we hide this thing?" Randy asked. "I've got a good place," I answered. "But run over to that copy center by the condo and make a few copies, and then bring them back and I'll take care of the original."

While Randy took off to make copies, I went back into the condo and made a phone call. I took the card that the cab driver had given me the night before and dialed his number. A groggy voice answered the phone and I asked, "Is this Carl?" "Yes. Who is calling?" he answered. "Its James Bond from last night. Do you remember me?" I asked. "Of course I do," he said. "What's up?" "I have an acting job. Are you interested?" "Yes sir," he said. "Are you working today?" I continued. "Only if I want to, because I own my own cab," he replied. "Well Carl, here is a chance for your first academy award," I said. "I'm ready. What do you want me to do?" he asked.

"Do you remember that woman in the limo last night?" "How could I not. That's about the most beautiful creature I've ever seen." "Would you recognize her if you saw her again?" I continued. "Absolutely," he answered. "I need you to clean yourself up and go to the hotel and wait for her in the lobby. When you see her, I need you to get some information for me. First of all I need her room number, and if she checks out I need you to follow her and find out where she ends up. Have you got a camera on your cell phone?" I asked. "Of course," he answered. "Then if you see her with anyone else, I need a picture. But don't get caught because if you do you could be in real danger. Are you still in?" I asked. "Totally," he answered. "Then get your butt out of bed and get over there. If you learn anything give me a call," I continued. "I will Mr. Bond. I'm on my way."

There was a tap at the door and in walked Randy. "Turn on the TV," he said. "You are back in the headlines, Philly." I turned to CNN and within a few seconds my face was on the screen. We sat as the reporter told of my attempted escape from prison and that after searching the area around the institution and finding no evidence of my whereabouts that it was possible I had returned to the New York area. There had begun a nationwide search for me and I was identified as armed and dangerous. Everything else centered on the fact that several of the Arab states had now stopped all oil exports to the U.S. because of the bombing. The stocks on Wall Street were already starting to fall with the anticipated increase of gas at the pump here in the United States.

"Here is my phone," Randy said. And you get rid of it because I'm sure if they haven't been to my place already, they will be there soon. I've got to get to work before they find out I'm late. To be honest Philly, I'm a little scared." "I don't blame you," I replied. "But just keep your cool and everything will work out. You've been a huge help to me so far but don't even think about contacting me until this thing is over." "By the way, here is another $500.00 for you," Randy said. "I don't think you will be able to use my debit card anymore." "You are right," I answered. "Here it is," I said, handing it back to him. "So much for my mattress money," Randy laughed. "I wasn't expecting to support two people at my young age." I walked over and gave him a hug and he was off to work. I went back to the TV and knowing that for the next few weeks I was a marked man.

Without Randy to help as much anymore, I was left in a quandary. I knew he could still contact me on my cell phone when he was at work and I still felt he wasn't in danger. We had covered our tracks pretty good and there was no way that the feds could know that he could have contacted me.

My next step was crucial to uncovering this plot against me and finding the real motive behind my being set up. I turned on Tim's computer. I guess because he lived alone, he had never locked his information. I first went to his documents and found his schedule. I looked and noticed that he would be arriving home on this coming Saturday. That just gave me a couple of days to gather more evidence. I was taking a calculated risk in believing that Tim might help me if I had enough evidence to show him I was innocent. In the meantime, I had to get some information on Selene and how she fit into the picture.

FINDING SELENE

My cell phone rang and I noticed it was Carl. "Hi. How is my favorite actor?" I asked. "I'm good," he replied. "I saw Selene this morning when she came down for breakfast. She ate alone and then left the building. I followed her and she went shopping just down the block from the hotel. I then followed her back to the hotel. I got in the elevator ahead of her and pushed the twenty first floor button. A moment later she walked in and I said, Hi, what floor?" She said, twenty-one. And I said, That's my floor as well." "We never said anything all the way up to the top floor and I let her exit the elevator first." "Have a nice day," I said. And she responded, "You too." "She turned right and started down the hall. I turned to the left and started the other way. I walked slowly and then pretended to fumble, looking for my keys as I stood at the door of one of the rooms. I saw her stop, bring out her card and enter her room. I waited a minute and then went down the hall and got her room number. It is room number 2108 and it says 'executive suite' on the door."

"Fantastic. "Where are you now?" I asked. "I'm in the lobby again wondering if there is anything else you want me to do." "What are the chances of you getting inside her room?" I asked. "If I knew what time they made up the room and if she left, I could probably get in," he answered. "What am I looking for?" Carl asked. "I really don't know," I replied. "I just need some information on who she is and what she is doing here." "I hope I'm getting well paid for this," Carl replied. "Don't worry about that," I said. "I promise it will be worth it for you. Just see what you can come up with," I continued. "And I'll get back to you later on."

I spent the rest of the day charting what had happened so far and where I was going from here. I fell asleep on the couch. I woke to my cell phone and saw it was nearly 8:00 o'clock. Once again it was Carl and he had some more news for me. "That limo we followed yesterday came and picked up the girl again and I followed them to a big building on the east side of the city. The place looked like a mansion to me but had a big driveway and a security gate. I'm assuming it was some body's home. I got as close as I could and got a couple of pictures of the two guys that were with the girl as they got out of the Limo. One of the men was the same guy we followed but the other I had never seen before." "Can you e-mail me those pictures?" I asked. "Sure. I'll send them in a minute," he answered. "Oh and can you include an address?" I continued. "Sure. They are on the way," he said and hung up.

"Carl, you've had a long day. Why don't you go get some rest and I'll call you tomorrow." "Sounds good to me," he replied. "Someone is going to recognize my cab one of these times and I won't be able to follow anyone." "Good job Carl. I'll talk to you later."

A minute later I got the pictures. Sure enough, Selene and the guy from yesterday were the same, but the third guy was hard to make out. I tried to zoom in a bit and there he was. It was none other than Dr. Walker in the flesh. Things were coming together and I wrote down the events of the day so I wouldn't forget them. I went back to the computer and typed in the address that Carl had given me. It was the Venezuelan Embassy, and as I continued my research, the photo of that South American Ambassador appeared on my screen. I instantly recognized him as the person with the girl in the Limo. Things were starting to make even less sense to me at that point. What did Dubai, Venezuela, and the United States have in common.

Then it hit me. "How stupid are you Chambers," I said to myself. "It's got to be oil." I had noticed that the price of gas in the US had been in that $4.00 range, but with the unrest in the Arab world we all assumed that gas could go over $6.00 or $7.00. I knew that some way this all had to be connected, but it wouldn't overturn my case unless I found out who was involved. I knew that that might not be the reason, but it sure looked like it was a great possibility.

When I woke the next morning I rolled over in bed, grabbed the remote and turned on the TV. "Oh good," I thought. "another bombing." This time it was in Kuwait, and once again some of their diplomats were killed. Naturally, since I had possibly escaped, it would be easy to tie me to another disaster. Right on cue my name came up with the information that I had been tied to an anti-Islam group while in college. I knew where that had come from and of course, naturally the source was from the office of my professor, Dr. Walker. "Here we go again," I thought as the vivid shots of the bombing kept flashing across the screen. The group that had set me up was at it again and doing a very good job.

I hadn't heard from Randy for quite a while and the thought of that was driving me crazy. I had to go to his house and see what was happening. I grabbed the keys off the wall and headed to the basement. I got in the Escalade, pushed the remote and headed out of the garage and onto the street.

As I approached Randy's house I could see a couple of cars that seemed to be suspicious. I drove right past his house and could see there was some activity inside. I parked about a block away and began to jog toward Randy's home. I had borrowed some of Tim's sweats and sneakers, so I wouldn't seem to stand out. As I jogged by the house I saw a neighbor two doors down anxiously looking toward the home. I kept jogging on the spot and asked what was going on. The older man told me that a group of, what looked like FBI agents, had come in the night before and taken his neighbor, Randy down for questioning. While he was gone the neighbor said, another vehicle arrived and several people entered his home. I tried to get a little closer, but they said for me to stay away and it was government business. "Did the guy ever return?" I asked. "Oh yes, he came back a few hours later, but something is going on over there because Randy's been in there the whole time this morning. He's a nice kid," the neighbor went on. I would find it hard to believe he's done anything wrong. "Well, thanks for the update," I said and continued jogging down the block and back to the car. There was nothing I could do and I was sure there was nothing they could pin on him so I got in the car and headed back toward town.

I needed to get my head thinking about something else so I picked up the phone and called Lisa. "Hi," I said. "it's John." Sorry about the other night." "That's all right. Did you figure out what you had?" she asked. "Just the one day flu I guess, because after I went home and got to sleep I felt much better the next morning. Hey, what time do you get off work?" I asked her. "Four thirty," she answered. "How about going to a movie?" I asked. "That would be great." "Where should I pick you up?" I asked. She gave me her address and I said, "I'll put it on the GPS and I will see you at say 7:00 o'clock." "That would be great," she answered.

I picked her up and opened the door for her. "Nice wheels," she said. "But a little big for a single guy." "Oh, didn't I tell you I have a wife and three kids back home," as I climbed in beside her. "Shut up," she said, and punched me in the arm. It was a great night and we enjoyed a burger and a movie. For the first time in a couple of months, I just relaxed and enjoyed the company of one very pretty woman. When we arrived back at her place she said, "Do you want to stay for a while?" I said, "I'd better not. My boss is arriving at the airport tomorrow and I've got some book work to do before he gets here. I'll call you after he leaves, and if you invite me in again you might never get rid of me," I laughed. She came toward me and wrapped her arms around my shoulders. I hugged her and said, "You feel really good." "Do I really want to leave?" I thought to myself. "Hey Lisa, I really do need to go, but I had a great time," I said as I broke away. "I'll see you on Monday."

When I got back I turned on the TV and turned to Fox News. It was still all about the bombing and the angry threats that were coming from the Middle East directed at the United States. I turned off the TV and started to clean up my mess. I still wasn't sure how I was going to approach Tim, but I knew that I needed him if I was to ever clear myself. I hoped I was reading Tim correctly, because if I wasn't my life as a free man was finished.

Saturday morning I got up and washed the sheets and pillowcases that were on Tim's bed. I vacuumed and cleaned all the dishes. When I arrived at the condo his place was spotless, and it needed to be that way when he returned. During the last day and a half I had assembled a note book which I was going to leave on Tim's table. It started with a letter from me asking him to look at the information before he did anything or called anyone.

The first page of the booklet was a copy of the transfer we had taken off the window in the lawyer's office, with an explanation of what it was, and it showed that the office truly was there and that I worked there.

The next three pages were pictures of the people I had told Tim about in detail, including Selene and Dr. Walker. It explained who they were, their titles and who they were with. I also said that the pictures had been taken during the last few days, right here in New York.

The next page was a list of my two account numbers, which supposedly, had all the money I had received for assisting in the bombing. I said if you will check, you will see they have a zero balance.

The final page was a note that told him to look in his closet, and there he would find his winter jacket that I had borrowed from him at the prison.

By now he would know that I had truly escaped and had been in his condo. The letter went on to say that, in the eyes of the law you have:

1. Helped me escape from your prison.
2. Given me your jacket so I could make my escape without freezing.
3. Allowed me to use your apartment as a hide out.
4. Let me borrow your clothes, your computer and your phone while I have been evading authorities in New York.
5. Allowed me to use your vehicle whenever I wanted.
6. Willingly gave me the keys to your apartment.

I concluded with one final statement:

Tim, either you are guilty of helping a terrorist, or you have been framed! All I ask is that you pick up the cell phone which I left on your night stand, call me and let me show you the evidence that I have which shows that I am innocent and that I too have been framed. You are probably the only person who can help me prove my innocence. Just push the redial button! If I don't hear from you in the next few minutes, I will never bother you again or implicate you. Hopefully you will never see me again, especially in your prison. Thanks—Phil

TIM'S RETURN

I waited outside the condo anticipating the arrival of Tim. It was dark when a cab pulled up and I saw Tim get out of the car and head for the building. I watched as he buzzed himself in and headed for his apartment. I followed him into the building and then up to his floor. I waited at the end of the hall, not knowing if he would call me or the FBI.

It was probably fifteen minutes and finally the phone rang. I answered it and said, "Hi Tim, are you in shock?" "Yes, to put it mildly," he said. "Will you help me?" I asked. "Yes I will," he replied. "I promise I will. Where are you?" Tim asked. "I'm right here," I said as I opened the door to his apartment. "I'm right here."

We just stood there facing each other, both of us unsure how to act. Tim broke the silence and said, "You are one amazing man, Phillip Chambers. I don't know how you did it but I'm looking forward to finding out." I reached out and shook his hand. "It's a long story," I said but it's far from over. Let's sit down and talk."

For the next few hours I told him everything that had happened. He sat in amazement as I told him of the escape, finding Selene, and collecting information that would clear me. When I finished my travelogue I said, "What is important is where we go from here." "I agree," answered Tim. "But I need to know a few important things first. You didn't wear my underwear did you?" "No," I answered, but just about everything else," I laughed. "Let me ask you something," I said. "Ok shoot. What do you want to know?" Tim asked. "When did you realize that I had escaped?" I asked. "When I walked into my condo and read your information," he answered. "Hey," he continued. "They are not even sure yet where you went to or if you are frozen somewhere in the wilderness. "Then why am I on the news still, and why did they question my buddy Randy?" "Hey, they had virtually no leads and they sure never broke your kiddy code on your e-mail," he laughed.

"So, what do you want me to do?" Tim asked. "I want you to find the real bad guys and take them up North with you," I answered. "You are one of the only people on the planet who can access files inside the FBI or secret service. Just tell them that you want to find me and you are not stopping until you do," I continued. "I need to know information on the guys in these pictures and who their associates are." "Well, tomorrow I'll start investigating, but right now I'm real tired," Tim said. "And by the way, can I have my bed back?" he laughed

The next morning we ate some breakfast and discussed what to do for the day. I asked Tim if he would check up on what was happening with Randy and see if they had anything on him. He said he would and then would get busy and start uncovering whatever he could. "The main thing I want you to do today is to get some information on the girl named Selene, and another girl that works for the real estate company that rented the building to my law firm." "What's her name?" He asked.

"Lisa Conrad," I replied, holding up the picture that I had taken of both girls. "Wow, those are two foxy ladies," Tim said. "Can I have one or do you want them both?" he asked. "Do a good job and I'll line you up," I laughed. "Take that picture and run it through your machines that can find these women. Take this cell phone that Randy bought me because there is no way to trace any calls. Let me know if you find anything out," I continued.

"I have the highest security, so I should be able to find out anything I need to. I'm the last person they would ever suspect," he chuckled. "Remind me again why I'm working for you?" he asked. "Never mind," he answered himself. "I'm a sucker for watching the good guys win and the bad guys lose." Tim disappeared out the door and headed for the Bureau. I stayed home and continued to try and figure out the master plan behind the bombing.

About two o'clock I got a call from Tim. "Hey, I'm outside in the park across from the homeland security office. I checked out Lisa and she is legit. No affiliation with anyone sinister. I'm sure she is no part of the cover up. Now Selene is a different story. I barely put her in the computer when two agents came over to me." "Who are you looking for?" the older guy said. I told them who I was and that I was checking every lead to find you. "I thought she might be involved with the escape of Chambers," I said. "My name is Tim, and I'm the guy in charge of the great Northern Prison where Chambers seems to have escaped," I said and held out my hand. "My name is Kramer and this is my partner, Agent Johnson." "Good to meet you guys," I said. "Do you have any information on this girl named Selene?" I asked.

"We do have some information, but we are not sure how she is involved in this case. She obviously knows Chambers and we have someone at her hotel watching her. We also found out that her last name is Velez and she is from Venezuela. Her father evidently owns the biggest private oil company in the country but at this point is being held by the head of the army, with Mr. Velez and his wife in confinement. The country's leader has put his own guys in charge of the operation," Kramer continued. "Thanks guys," I replied. "That will save me a whole lot of time. Does she have any kind of a record?" I asked. "Nothing we could find," said Johnson. "But we do have some information that she was here in the country and staying in a nearby hotel." "Thanks again guys," I said. "Just keep me posted if you get any news about her. I doubt she has anything to do with Chambers anyway."

With that I told the guys I was going to lunch and I'm sure they bought my story. "Oh, on your friend Randy, he has been released for the time being. They found nothing in the e-mail connecting him to you. They have also questioned your mom and dad and they are convinced they have never heard from you."

RECRUITING SELENE

"What are you going to do today Phil?" Tim asked me. "I'm going to see Selene if I can. She just doesn't seem to fit in with those other guys and she must have a lot of information." I called my cabbie spy, Carl, and he is waiting to pick me up.

When he arrived, I told him the plan and gave him his assignment. I gave him $200.00 dollars and told him the rest would come later. "I want you to find the cartel guy and divert his attention when I go into the building." I waited for my cue and when Carl started making a fuss and the people in the lobby turned their heads, I walked into the hotel and headed to the house phone and calmly dialed room 2108.

A woman answered the phone and asked, "Who is calling?" "I am sorry to bother you Miss but we seem to be having a problem with the smoke alarm in your room. Is it making any kind of a sound?" I asked. "Just one minute," she said. "I'll check." She returned in a minute and said," I don't hear anything." "Our monitors are indicating a short in the wiring. When would be a good time to check on it?" I continued. "We certainly don't want to bother you." "I'm coming down in a few minutes to get some breakfast. You could come then," she said. "Then I'll send one of our men up right away and you can let them in when you are ready to leave. I'm sure it will take less than a minute to check it." "That would be fine," she said.

I waited a minute and then headed for the elevator. I waited for the door to open and turned right and proceeded to room 2108. I knocked gently on the door and said, "Hotel maintenance." "I'll be there in a minute came," the voice from inside. I reached into my pants and pulled out my small hand gun. She opened the door and said, "I was just leaving. I hope you find what you need." "I hate to do this to you but what I really want is to talk to you." I put the gun against her chest and pushed her back into the room.

"Please don't hurt me," she cried. "I've done everything you've asked and I haven't said anything to anyone, I promise." "I'm not going to hurt you. I just need to talk to you," I said. "Sit down on the chair and give me your purse," I said, trying to sound very authoritative. I took the purse and looked through it to see if she had a weapon or mace or a knife, but found nothing. I could tell by the tightness of her pants and halter top that she wasn't hiding any weapons under her clothes.

I put the gun back in my pants and sat down right beside her and said, "I just need some answers to a few questions and if I get the right answers, you may go." I could see she was very scared and shaking. "Have you ever seen me before?" I asked. "I think I saw you a few days ago in the restaurant," she said. "You were with another woman. "That's right," I said. "But I want you to look a little deeper and tell me if we have met before." Finally my eyes met hers and after a few moments she raised her hand to her mouth and gasped, "Mr. Chambers? But it can't be," she continued. "I mean, how did you escape from prison and how did you find me?" "I believe I was going to ask the questions, and I want a straight answer or you'll never leave this room alive," I said. "Do you understand?" She nodded her head in the affirmative.

"You obviously know my story, since you are involved in it up to your eye balls. I need to know why you set me up and who the people are you have been with the last couple of days," I continued. "Well, if I tell you the truth they will kill me, and if I tell a lie you will kill me, so what am I supposed to do?" she asked. "I've always been taught that telling the truth is the right thing to, do and if you do, I promise I will protect you," I replied.

Selene, I think you know I was framed, and I think you know the reason. I know who your parents are and that your last name is Velez," I continued. "I also know that you are being watched by the secret service and they have an agent posted in the lobby. I know you spent yesterday at the Venezuelan embassy with the ambassador and a Dr. Walker from Harvard University. If I'm going to clear myself, and you know I'm innocent, we will take care of you. That is assuming you are not involved," I concluded.

"I might as well tell you the whole story," she said. "A few months ago I was attending a business seminar her in New York. I have been the operations manager for my father's oil company the past two years. While I was here, the dictatorship in my country arrested my parents and charged my father with some sort of corruption charge, and said they would be taking over his business until they cleared things up. My father really has nothing to do with the day to day running of the business because that was my job," she continued. "I also have signing authority for all accounts. I had no idea what was going on down there until I received a call from the Venezuelan Ambassador to visit him at his Embassy. I was picked up from the hotel in a Limo and driven to his home on the embassy grounds."

"Once inside, I was informed of the situation, and that from now on I would be working for them. I was also told that if I didn't cooperate that my parents would somehow be killed in a tragic accident, and it would be in my best interest to do as I was told. Naturally there was nothing I could do but agree. I told them I would do whatever they needed as long as they left my parents alone."

"I was allowed to call and talk to my father, and he confirmed what had happened. They have treated me pretty good so far, knowing that I am the only one with the codes which open up the bank accounts and gives them access to the transportation of oil to America. You can see that put us both in a catch 22 situation. I told them that I would work with them if they would not keep me under any sort of house arrest. They agreed to let me stay in this hotel but monitor everything I do."

"My first assignment was to go to Dubai and give you a suitcase and directions to deliver it. At that point I had no idea what they were planning. After the bombing I knew exactly what had happened, and I became an accomplice in the case much like you were. They really set me up good and after the attack they knew they had my full attention and loyalty. If I said anything, I would go to jail as your accomplice. Now that the second bombing has occurred it's only a matter of days before the Middle East stops sending oil to America."

"For the past month the corrupt leaders in my country have been loading my father's tankers with fuel for the U.S. market. In a matter of days the price of oil is going to double and Venezuela will be the country that brings in billions of dollars. Currently my country has been struggling financially, and so this well-managed diversion will work out perfect for them and those involved will become instant millionaires."

I listened intently as her story unfolded before me. "I guess that includes my old professor, Dr. Walker," I said. "I was the perfect guy for him because he knew I trusted him and would call him if I got into any trouble. He really played me," I continued. "And I fell for it hook, line and sinker."

"Well, I guess we need to figure out where to go from here," I said. "I'll have the people on my side get you out of this mess if you trust me." "Do I have a choice?" she asked. "Of course you do, and you have your parents' lives at stake. I know that we will have the ability to free your parents if you join us and help bring these guys down." "How do you intend to do that?" she asked. "There are many people in your government that are part of this." "Do you know who they are?" I asked. "No," she replied. "But I could identify them if you showed me a picture. I have been at the embassy when they have had meetings there."

"I have an idea and I hope it will work," I said. "I want to run it by my partners so, in the meantime, you will just have to continue to play along with these guys. Have they done anything to get the codes from you except threaten you with your parents?" I asked. "No," she answered. "But I know that some of your senators have already approved the buying of our oil and the shipments are to start immediately. I also heard them say that the funds for the oil would be released as soon as the oil arrives on American soil. I am assuming that oil will cost over $200.00 a barrel and my country will be the only one which can supply your country with the oil that America needs."

"Well, I guess you and I have become partners. I am sorry about the gun but I really didn't know where you stood on this thing. It will be hard for us to communicate, so from now on I want you to talk to me through one of our guys. His name is Carl, and he is a cab driver." I took his card from my wallet and gave it to her. "If there is any information you need to get to me, just call him and he'll take care of you. He has my cell phone number and he can get you in touch with me but don't call me unless you are in that cab." "Alright," she said. "I guess we'll both have to trust each other."

"I'd better go," I said as I stood up from the couch. "I never imagined we would be in the same situation when we first met a month or so ago. I promise I will do everything I can to get this case solved and get your parents to safety." I squeezed her hand as I walked away and headed for the door. I sighed as she closed the door behind me. It was good to know that this ravishing woman was not one of the bad guys.

I climbed back into the cab and told Carl about Selene and that she would be contacting him and she'll want to use your cell phone when she needs to get a hold of me. "So she's alright?" Carl asked. "She's more than alright," I laughed. "She's perfect. He drove me back to the condo and I invited him in. So far he didn't have a clue of what was going on but it was time to let him know a little bit. I gave him only a tidbit but promised him that it would be worth it once we solved the case. He left just as Tim arrived. I introduced him as the passed in the hall. "Hi Carl, It's nice to have a getaway man," Tim laughed. "Great to have a guy like you on our side."

We decided to put our story on the wall in the bedroom. We hung things up on the wall and talked about what was ahead of us. I told Tim about Selene and the story he gave me matched hers. "Where do we go from here?" I asked. "I think the best thing we do is get rid of you." "What are you talking about?" I asked. "Well, the fact is no one knows where you are and if you are still alive. So I was thinking it was time to kill you," Tim said. "Hand me the coat you stole from me." I walked over, picked it up and handed it to him. "Now take this knife and cut yourself," he continued. "What are you talking about?" I asked. "I need some blood on this coat to show you died in the wilderness," Tim answered.

I took one of my razor blades and cut myself and then wiped it on the jacket. "That blood looks pretty good, but give me some more," he laughed. I did it and then asked how he was going to pull this off. "I'm going to ship this back in a box on the next plane, and have it delivered to the Warden. I will send him a note telling him that one of the search party found it about 30 miles away, landed his chopper, picked it up and brought it to me," he continued. "Is he going to buy that?" I asked. "Why wouldn't he? They have your DNA on file and everything on it is yours," he answered. "Besides, it was me who was in charge of your search. At least they will stop looking for you for a while if they think you are dead."

"What else did you find out today?" I asked. "Someone needs to get some information on that guy at the Embassy and on your teacher, Dr. Walker," Tim answered. If what you said about Randy is true and he's no longer a suspect, then he's the perfect man for the job," I answered. "He's way up there in Google and has access to a lot of things." "That's great, and in the meantime you need to ask your girlfriend what she really knows about those renters and if she doesn't, would she be willing to get us some information," Tim concluded.

RECRUITING LISA

I invited Lisa out for dinner, and after eating I invited her up to the condo. I unlocked the door and we walked inside. Sitting on the couch was Tim, who looked very relaxed, just sitting there watching TV. I'm sure Lisa wasn't expecting anyone being there but the two of us.

"This is my roommate, Tim," I said to Lisa. They shook hands and she sat on the chair facing him. "Lisa, this is going to seem really weird to you but I want you to trust us," I said. "Tim, please tell Lisa about herself." Tim started right in and told her where she was born, where she was from, the name of her high school, her university, her family, her favorite actor, favorite food until she knew that Tim knew everything about her. "What is going on here?" while looking very anxious. "One thing I never mentioned was the fact that you took law enforcement in school and haven't found a job in your field yet. Is that right?" asked Tim. "Yes, but how can you know all that?" she replied. "Well, this is kind of a job interview," Tim answered. "Are you interested in furthering your career"? he asked.

"Yes I am, but do you two know how strange this seems?" she asked. "Well, I work with the FBI and I am currently in charge of the newest, most modern prison in the world. Phil has been telling me about you and thought you might be interested in getting out of that real estate office and doing what you love." "Sounds interesting," she answered. "But tell me more, or are you guys pulling my chain?" Tim reached over and grabbed his FBI identification and showed it to her. I tried to look away from the glares I was getting from Lisa. "No I'm serious," Tim continued. "And I'm going to need you right away." "Depends on what you pay," she laughed. "Come with me," Tim said as he walked toward his bedroom. "You want me to follow you, someone I met ten minutes ago, and into your bedroom?" she asked. "I know it looks bad," I piped in. "Just come with me," I said reaching out to her and pulling her off the chair.

As we entered the room, she saw the collage of things on the wall. "This is the case we are working on right now." She walked over and began looking at the notes and pictures on the wall. "Are you familiar with this?" Tim asked. "Yes," she replied. "Everyone in the world knows about this case." "Well, there is a lot more to this than first meets the eye," he continued. "I thought this guy was captured, admitted to the bombing and he is in jail, or by some reports, dead.

"Well, I'm not dead," I said. "Take a closer look at the picture, get rid of the beard and see if you recognize me." She looked at the picture, then back at me then back at the picture. "How can this be?" she asked. "Well, come back in the living room and we will tell you the entire story," I answered.

For the next hour we told Lisa the entire story and what had happened. She sat in amazement as we finished the story. "Lisa, understand that we have done a complete background check on you and we want your help," said Tim. "It was a fluke that Phil even found you," he continued. "Phil needed to get some information about the renters over on 5th Avenue and ended up with you being the real estate agent. Once I arrived back in town and found out America's most wanted was sleeping in my bed, I had to do something. He told me the same story we just told you and I told him I would help solve this case. He showed me the picture of you two at the restaurant and we knew we needed more information. Between Randy and I, we did a search on you and found out your background. So here we are and, if you choose, you have gone from desk jockey to undercover agent," Tim concluded.

"Well naturally I'm shocked," Lisa said. "I can't believe this is real." "Phil has put his complete trust in you and we want you as part of our team," Tim said. "Are you in?" Tim continued. "I'm in," she answered. "I've always wanted to do something like this. "When do I start?" "Tomorrow morning," he replied. "I need all the information you can get on the group that rented that office from your company. I need names, pictures, and the names of owners of the real estate company you work for."

"After you get what we need, tell them that you just got another job offer in your field, and you will be leaving in a few days," Tim concluded. "I always knew there was something wrong about that company and that building. I was told it was very private and I shouldn't talk to anyone about it. I was told by my boss, in no uncertain terms, should I ever even mention it to anyone. I promised not to and that is why he let me show it to Phil because all the evidence was gone and there was nothing left to tell," she told us.

By now it was getting late and I said," I better get this girl home. She's got a lot of work to do tomorrow." "Let me do that," Tim said. "I'd like to drive my own car just once," he said. "I hope you haven't broken anything." "OK," I said. "But make sure you kids don't stay out too late,"

I laughed. "Don't worry about us and don't stay up and wait for me," he laughed back at me.

I sat down, after they left, and thought about what had happened. I analyzed what was happening and the cast of characters to solve the mystery.

1. I had just put complete trust in a girl (Lisa) who I barely knew.
2. I had recruited an actor (Carl) who was moonlighting as a cab driver.
3. I had given away my identity to a girl (Selene) who had helped frame me and sent me to prison.
4. I had confided in and sought help from the man (Tim) who was in charge of the prison I just came from.
5. I had put my best friend (Randy) in a position that could land him in jail or dead.

And then there is me, a convicted terrorist and murderer, who either died in Northern Canada, or is one of the world's most wanted criminals.

Little did they know what was lying ahead for each of them. We needed proof of the conspiracy and enough evidence to get the real criminals into jail in my place. My head was spinning, as I thought of what was happening, and how solve the situation.

Selene was the one person I couldn't get off my mind. Not just her beautiful face, but the prospect that we had put her and possibly her family in great peril. But deep inside I felt calm and comfortable that justice would prevail, and I would once again be a free man. Finally, I fell asleep and never even heard Tim return to the condo.

The next morning the phone rang and it was Selene calling on Carl's cell phone. She had pretended to go shopping and Carl had picked her up with his cab. She told me that she was to be picked up and taken to the Embassy that night to discuss some things that had happened in the past twenty-four hours. "Just find out as much information as you can and get back to me tomorrow morning," I said. I went on to say that I assumed they were going to put some heavy pressure on her to relinquish her banking information so they could access the funds she had control of. I also tried to explain that this pressure would come with more threats of torture or death to her parents. I concluded by telling her to keep her cool and tell them that she would not give them any information unless they brought her parents to New York and united them with her. She said she would, and hung up the phone.

The news on every station on TV was about the price of gas. The Middle East had shut off the gas flow to America because of the bombings and the price of gas was skyrocketing. The news also showed that a person had been arrested in connection with the second bombing in Kuwait. Once again, it was an American who had been charged with terrorism and murder just as I had been in the first case.

I called Tim who was already at the bureau doing his homework on the case. I asked him to check out the new bombing suspect and see how similar it was to my situation. He called me back about an hour later, telling me that it was very similar to my case. He was also an ex-Harvard lawyer working for a law firm in Washington, who pleaded innocence just as I had. Tim had the perfect cover to get information on this latest bombing because he was sure this new guy would be heading to his prison just as I had.

Naturally the TV and newspapers were indicating that both bombings were connected and that both the new suspect and I were part of an anti-Muslim plot, looking for revenge for past attacks against Americans. A minute later I saw my face appear on CNN telling everyone that my blood-stained Jacket had been found and that I was possibly dead after running away from the northern prison. That was good news for me because if I were presumed dead I could move around more freely and help with the case. I spent the rest of the day trying to figure out our next move. I knew that with the Embassy contacting Selena that things were about to happen and fast.

That night we arranged for a meeting at Tim's condo with every one on our team excluding Selene. One by one they arrived until everyone was present. It was time to update everyone on the entire situation and get their thoughts on what the solutions were. Randy was first to give us information. "I did a lot of research on Dr. Walker and the Embassy guy and found some real interesting things," he said. "Dr. Walker has a lot of connections in Washington with both Senators and Congressmen. Interestingly enough, almost all of them are on oil and trade committees. This thing is a lot deeper and more dangerous than any of you can imagine," he continued. "I'm afraid many in Washington are up to their eyeballs in this."

Speaking of eye balls, I thought Carl's might pop right out of his head as he listened to our stories and what was happening. Randy had also done a thorough search on Carl as well, and we were very sure that we had a great spot for him as we went forward. Carl remained quiet but we could all tell he was overwhelmed with all of the information.

Next we heard from Lisa, who had been working that day to find out information on the rental and the partners in her realty company. "It was difficult to access as much as I wanted with someone over my shoulder at work," she said. "I did find a couple of really interesting things that really will put things in perspective," she suggested. "You probably figured out by now that there was never a rental agreement made between our company and the legal firm. I did, however, find the deposit for the rental and a copy of the check signed by a Mr. Kahlid Ampour. I'm not sure if that is his real name but I also wrote down the account number and here it is," she said as she handed the paper to Tim. I couldn't help but notice a connection between Tim and Lisa every time they looked at each other but maybe I was just imagining things.

Lisa went on to say that the amount paid to her real estate company was ten times what was usually paid for a rental like that one. She also pointed out that only the president of her company had anything to do with the transaction. "I also noticed that my boss had ordered furniture for the entire office from a rental firm. In the memo I found he indicated a floor plan and designated office space for each of the people who were to work there. If you look closely at the document you will see KH at one desk and PC at another. Also shown are the words secretary, and steno with the other desks. Phil, did you ever see anyone else in the office except for Mr. Z and the other two girls?" Lisa asked. "I only saw them in the office, although I was interviewed and ate dinner with Mr. Foreman, but I was told he was in a different office." "That makes sense then," Lisa continued. "Would you recognize Mr. Foreman if you saw him again?" Phil asked? "I know I would," she answered. "I was with him for a couple of hours. I am going to assume there is no Mr. Foreman, but with the account number and the names I gave you, hopefully something important will turn up." Once again she handed more information to Tim. "Thanks Lisa," I said. "That police training you got in college finally seems to be put to good use," I laughed. "Tim, what have you got for us?" I asked.

"I have searched everything I could about the Embassy," Tim said. "I cross-referenced the picture of the man in the picture and he is the ambassador to America. His name is Eduardo Palma. From what I could see he is a longtime aide to the president. He is also, a childhood friend and served as the chief of police in the capital. He was accused of being very brutal and considered one of the most feared men in Venezuela. His nick name was the butcher, and his police force was considered the most corrupt in all of South America. Because of his closeness to the president he was given this assignment here in the United States. With things going the way they are, it is no surprise he is involved in this. I'm not sure if the President is involved in this, but I wouldn't be surprised."

"I also noticed that the Embassy is heavily guarded, which is a bit unusual for here in America," Tim continued. "If Selene is given some sort of ultimatum tonight, and she follows through with the plan I gave her, we will need to act fast," I interrupted. "She will call me in the morning and we can make plans on where we go from here. If everything turns out the way I think it can, Selene's parents will be on a plane here tomorrow. I assume they will keep them at the Embassy until she gives them the information they want and then they will get rid of all of them. I know that Selene will lose her freedom once her parents arrive. I have a plan to get them out," I continued. "But I will need everyone's help. We will meet back here tomorrow night and I will outline our duties then."

Every one began to leave and Tim offered to walk Lisa to the parking garage. I looked out the door as they walked down the hall and just as they came to the stairwell, I saw her reach out and take Tim's hand in hers. "Wow," I thought to myself. "That was fast!" But it didn't bother me because, in actual fact, they looked pretty good together. When it came to women, I had thoughts of no one but Selene for the past few days. I knew I had to keep my focus and if Selene was interested in me there had been no indication by her.

Tim came back about fifteen minutes later and I asked him if Lisa had a hard time getting her car started. "No," he answered. "We were just chatting." "Is that why you have lipstick on your collar?" I asked. As soon as he glanced down, I knew I had him. He turned a little red and started to say he was sorry, but I cut him off and said, "Hey, I was just kidding, but I got you didn't I!" "Don't worry about it Tim. She's a real nice girl and I think you two look great together," I continued. "You mean you are not angry that I like her?" he replied. "I don't mind at all," I said. "Just don't fall in love till we get this thing finished. I'm going to sleep," I said. "We'll see you in the morning."

THE EMBASSY ESCAPE

The phone rang again and I was anxious to hear Selene's voice on the other end. "I've only got a few minutes Phil, but let me get you up to date on what happened last night. There were a few men in the room when I arrived and the mood was clearly different as I entered. Up to this point they had been fairly good to me and trusted I wouldn't try to escape because of my parents. They told me they wanted the information now or they would kill my Mom and Dad. I did what you suggested and told them that they could have all of my information once I was reunited with my parents. They had no choice except to agree, and said they would fly them in later today. In fact, they should be on the plane right away," she continued.

"Phil," she went on. "I'm really scared. They let me stay at the hotel last night but said they are coming at noon to get me and that I will be staying at the Embassy from now on. I was lucky and got a hold of Carl and he's driving me shopping right now. In a couple of hours I won't be able to contact you again." "Don't worry," I answered. "Do you know which airline they will be on?" I asked. "I'm not sure but they will be flying out of Caracus and arriving late this afternoon," she replied. "Do you know the limo service they use to pick you up?" I asked. "I think it is Lincoln Limo," she replied. "Do you always have the same driver?" I asked. "No, I've had a couple of different ones," she answered. "So if Carl is driving the Limo when they pick up your parents it won't seem out of the ordinary?" I continued. "I don't think so," she answered.

"Let me give you some advice as to what to do," I said. "Do you know where the bedrooms are in the Embassy?" I asked. "They are all upstairs," she said, and I know where they will put me," she continued. Because that was where they kept me until they seized my parents." "Which way does your bedroom window face?" I asked. "I'm not sure of the direction but its right across from a park," she answered. "Once the Limo arrives with your parents, make sure that you tell them that they need some time to unpack and freshen up. Also tell them that you want to be able to spend some time with them. Finally, we don't know where they will put your parents so when you ask to visit them, make sure that they come to your room, OK.?" "Alright," she answered. "I will do that."

"We are going to try and get some of our people into the Embassy and hopefully to your room. When the Limo arrives with Carl as the driver, will he be asked to bring your parents suitcases up to their suite?" I asked. "Yes." she replied. "That's what they usually do." "Is there a back stairway to the upstairs" I asked. "Yes, it's at the end of the hall," she replied. "Do you know if there is an alarm on the door?" I continued. "Yes, but it's an emergency door and I'm sure it will open." "When Carl tells you to run, you do just that and get out of there. Make sure you are wearing shoes that you can move in and make sure your parents have the same type of footwear," I said.

"If you exit to your left you will see a gate, and I want you to go directly there. The gate will be open and I will be waiting in Carl's cab outside that gate. Do you understand?" I asked. "Yes I do," she replied.

"Don't worry. Everything is going to be fine," I said. "Just trust me," I continued. "I'm looking forward to seeing you again," Selene said. "I'm just praying that it all works out." "Well, we don't have a backup plan and it is dangerous," I replied. "But we are going to make it work."

"We've arrived at the store, so I've got to go," she said. "I'm sure someone is following me." "Just play it cool," I said. "And get a different cab back to the hotel. Oh, and tell Carl to come to the condo as soon as he drops you off." "OK," she answered. "I owe you so much." "Don't worry. I'll collect once you and your family is safe," I laughed. She hung up the phone and was gone. I thought to myself, "Will I ever see her again?"

Tim had been listening to me and was trying to get something out of my conversation with Selene. As I hung up the phone he asked, "Sounds like you have a plan. Do you want to let me in on it?" "You are it," I said. "Here's what they have planned. I explained that he needed to get Lisa and Randy there right away. Each of the people in the group had an important part to play in our little game of escape.

Within an hour everyone had arrived. "We have no time to spare," I said. "Here is how the plan will work, and we only have one chance." I explained what was happening to everyone and then made the assignments.

1. "Tim, I need you to get on the computer and find out what time the plane arrives from Caracus, and if Selene's parents are on board. Is that possible?" I asked. "I have #1 security clearance, so that shouldn't be a problem." "Once you have that info, I need both you and Lisa to pick up the parents and get them into the limo out front. Carl, you will be driving that limo," I said.

2. "Randy, I need you to contact Lincoln Limo's and find out when a limo is booked for pick-up at the airport. How do we know they will be using a limo?" he asked. "That's their only mode of transportation," I answered, and that ambassador is arrogant enough that he will settle for nothing less. I then need you and Carl to go there and talk to the dispatcher. I don't know what it will cost, but offer him $1,000.00 if you have to and tell him that Carl needs to be the driver. Carl you will need to get a uniform from the dispatcher as well. Give him the money and tell him there will be another $1,000.00 when we return the Limo in a few hours. That way he won't say anything to anyone. That's probably more money than he makes in a month. The less he knows the better," I concluded. "Ok," they said. "We think we can handle that."

3. "Carl, as soon you get the four of them in the car, you are to drive directly to the Embassy. Once there, make sure you unpack the bags and ask the security guard where he wants you to take the luggage. Insist that is your job and you can lose your job if he tells you to leave the luggage anywhere except in their room."

4. "Tim and Lisa, I need you to look like the security bodyguards that have been assigned to bring Selene's parents to the Embassy," I said. "Can you get the uniforms and weapons and anything else you need to pass as the bodyguards?" I asked. "I think we can handle that," Tim replied. "And Lisa will finally get to wear a uniform," he laughed. "Tim, I also need you to have the real security guards that are accompanying the parents, to be detained by airport security. They need to be interrogated and sent back on the next plane or at least held overnight. Make sure you relieve them of all communication devices they might have at their disposal." "I think that I can handle that as well," he said. "And by the way, who is the corrections officer here,

you or me.?" I smiled at him and said, "Sorry, just trying to cover all the bases." "I'll get Kramer and Johnson to take care of that," Tim said. "You probably remember how good they are at interrogating someone, don't you?" "Only too well. They will be fine," I replied.

5. "Randy, once they are in, I need you to be the diversion. Get a couple of your buddies and go to the Embassy. You can start by following the limo inside and get in a political argument with the security guards. It's important that you look crazed and not all there, although that shouldn't be hard for you," I laughed. "Very funny," he said, making a crazy face. "Give our people a couple of minutes to get inside and upstairs and then start the fireworks. Have your friends start throwing the loudest stuff you can find including some smoke bombs. It needs to be as realistic as possible. I need enough confusion to get the people inside to come out and look. Keep it up as long as you can and then get out of there."

6. "Tim, Lisa and Carl, once you hear the commotion you need to take care of any security that is upstairs and then head for the stairs at the end of the hallway. Go downstairs and turn left. I will have the lock cut off the gate and I will be waiting in Carl's cab, across the street away from any security cameras. Get Selene, her parents and Carl into the cab and then head across the park where your Escalade will be waiting for you.

7. "Tim, I need you to have the federal authorities arrive and arrest those at the Embassy. I'm sure you can brief the agents on enough charges to get them to the county courthouse for questioning. I know it's going to end up in court, so in the meantime we need a safe house for these guys. With the amount of money and reputations at stake you know that there will be a lot of people looking for these guys." "My uncle and aunt have

a cottage on a lake just outside of the city," Phil said. They go south for the winter and we can stay there until things calm down." "Now, let's get to work," I said. "This has all got to happen in the next few hours. With that, everyone headed out the door to get there assignment done.

"I will be here on the cell if anything goes wrong. I'll be close by if you need me," he concluded.

A while went by before I heard from Tim. He told me the plane would be arriving about 6:00 PM, which helped give us a couple more hours. "Lisa and I will be at the airport, and I've got Kramer and Johnson who will be at the security gate to delay the bodyguards.

I decided that I would drive to the airport and wait inside to see how things would work out. I gave the parking attendant $20.00 so I could leave the Escalade parked in front while I waited. As I walked into the airport doors, I saw Carl in the limo waiting. I gave him a nod and he replied back with a touch of his hat. I was not sure if Kramer and his partner would recognize me, so I made sure I stayed a few yards away from the gate. Everything was going according to plan so far.

I could see the gate from my spot in the arrival area. It was an international flight and I knew they had to enter there. I watched with anticipation as the people began to file through the gate. I could see Kramer and Johnson standing just inside the gate waiting for our people to arrive. Just then I saw a couple emerge, followed by two heavy set guys who looked like security. The woman in front was very striking, dark hair with a tint of grey. I knew in an instant that was Selena's mother. She was followed by a fairly short man with glasses and grey hair. I assumed that would be her husband. The two burley men were almost attached to each of the couple. I knew they would have no weapons because of the planes security policy.

I watched Kramer walk over and confront the bodyguard that was leading the group. I couldn't hear anything but I could see him show the man his badge. He began talking in a loud voice to Kramer and at that point Johnson came to his side. I could see the second bodyguard trying to explain that the husband and wife were their prisoners and they responded by showing some documents to the agents. I could hear a bit of the conversation between the two groups, enough to know what they were saying. One of the bodyguards motioned toward their prisoners and I could hear Johnson indicating that they would be held in a waiting room while the two bodyguards were taken to be questioned. The first bodyguard became angry and started cursing the agents saying they had no right to detain them. "It won't be long," Kramer said as he led the men away.

No sooner were they out of sight than Tim and Lisa appeared and began talking to them. In a minute I noticed they had cleared security and were headed out the airport door to the awaiting limo. Carl opened the door, then took their luggage and put it in the trunk. I knew that Tim and Lisa would update the couple on the situation and explain the getaway. I returned to my car and proceeded to follow the limo on its way to the Embassy.

I called Tim on his cell and he informed me that Lisa was talking the couple through the set up. He said that the couple was quite fluent in English, which made the translation quite easy. I hung up the phone and then called Randy to tell him we were on the way. I sped ahead toward the Embassy and parked the Escalade on the other side of the park. I then proceeded across the grass until I saw Carl's cab in the parking lot.

I reached in the back seat and found the bolt cutters. I then proceeded across the street toward the Embassy. The pictures that Tim had shown me of the Embassy were very good. I knew from them exactly where the security cameras were, as I made my way along the fence to the back gate. When I got there I cut the lock off the gate and then returned to the cab to wait.

About five minutes later the limo pulled up to the gate. A security officer came out and stood by Carl's window. Carl rolled down the window and the officer said, "May I see your clearance papers please? Carl reached down beside him and produced the papers that the dispatcher had given him. The officer gave them back and then went to the window in the back of the limo. Tim rolled down his window and the officer said," "We have been expecting you," and then motioned to Carl to proceed through the gate. He pulled through the gate and up the circular driveway. He parked directly in front of the Embassy door, then exited the limo and walked around the car to open the door for his passengers. Tim was the first to get out, followed by Mr. Velez and then his wife. Lisa was the last to exit the limo. By this time Carl had gathered the bags and was waiting for his passengers to walk up the short flight of stairs to the front door.

I think Tim and Lisa were surprised at the number of security men that were at the compound. The man who seemed in charge greeted Mr. Velez at the top of the stairs and extended his hand. Mr. Velez declined to return the extended hand and simply asked, "Where is my daughter?" Tim then walked over to the man and said, "Here are your prisoners. Where would you like us to take them?" Just follow my assistant and he will take you to their rooms. "Did you have any trouble with them?" he asked Tim. "None at all," he replied. "I will take them to their rooms and come back and see you in a couple of minutes," Tim continued.

The assistant reached down to take the bags, but Carl said, "I have them. "There are only four and they are all small." The assistant then walked through the door and up the staircase toward the second floor, followed by his entourage. They proceeded to the room to the right of the stairs which was just down the hall from the room where Selene was staying. The assistant reached in his pocket, produced a key and opened the door. The Velez couple walked in, followed by the assistant. "I hope this will be fine for you," he added.

At that moment Tim produced his gun and hit the assistant over the head, knocking him unconscious instantly. Lisa then flipped the bedroom light on, which was the signal for Randy and his crew to begin their assault on the Embassy. In less than thirty seconds there was a loud boom, followed by several more. Tim peered out the window and saw the court yard being filled with smoke and said, "Let's go!" Selene had heard the explosion and opened her door to see Lisa standing in the hall. "Selene," she said. "Let's go." Selene and her parents almost ran into each other as they left their room. Selene grabbed her Mom and was pushed down the hall by Tim and Carl. They went down the hall and onto the back stairs. They could hear yelling at the bottom of the foyer as they pushed open the door to the outside. Someone from the front yelled, "Check the prisoners upstairs." As soon as the door opened, the security alarm went off, and they headed for the gate running across the lawn as fast as they could. Tim and Lisa had a hold of Mrs. Velez and Carl was running beside Selene and her father. They ran through the gate and headed for the cab, which was across the street. The car engine was running and all the doors were open as they arrived. Phil was waiting and helped them into the car. Carl headed for the driver's side and in a matter of a few seconds the cab screamed out of the parking lot and onto the road. Tim grabbed Lisa by the hand and ran across the park to where his vehicle was waiting.

The Velez family members were crying as they hugged each other. "Is every one OK?" asked Phil? "Yes, we are fine," said Selene as she reached forward and kissed Phil on the cheek. Just then Carl said, "Get down. We have company. In his rear view mirror he could see headlights closing fast on the cab. "Hang on," he said. "Those idiots are not going to catch us. Get your seat belts on. This could be one crazy ride. Phil withdrew his gun from the holster in the back of his pants. Just then there was the sound of gunfire from the truck behind them. "Can you ditch them?" Phil asked. "Just watch me," Carl responded. "No one knows this city and it's streets like I do."

The cab swerved and headed down a dimly lit street, which seemed to head to nowhere. As he continued, the cab neared a commercial area. By now the truck was closer and shots rang out as one of the bullets caromed off the back of the cab. Carl quickly turned right behind a big metal building and then quickly right again and into what looked to be a warehouse. He never slowed down as the truck missed a second turn, not seeing where Carl had gone. A second later we heard the screeching of tires and then a loud crash. "That should take care of them," Carl said, as he sped through the warehouse, out the other side and back on down the back road. He then turned back onto the freeway toward Phil's uncle's cabin.

The cab arrived at the cabin, and Phil and Carl opened the doors for the Velez family. As Selene exited from her side of the car, she wrapped her arms around Phil and he happily returned the gesture. "How can we ever thank you?" she said, as a tear ran down her cheek. "It's a long way from over," I replied. "But for now let's get inside." Selene's mother and father really didn't know what had happened as they followed Phil into the home.

Once inside the house Phil welcomed everyone and shook hands with the mother and father. "I'm sure this seems crazy, but the most important thing is that you are safe for the moment. Carl said, "I need to get the car in the garage. I'm sure they will be looking for it. You don't see a lot of yellow cabs out here," he laughed. He walked out the door to park the car. Phil then had every one sit down and started to tell the story of what had happened.

A few minutes later his cell rang and it was Tim. "What happened?" Phil asked. "Well, Lisa and I went back to the Embassy and waited for the police to arrive. They were there just a couple of minutes after you got away. There was some gunfire from inside the Embassy gates but it subsided in a few minutes and the FBI agents entered the building," he continued. "A short time later some of the agents came out with a couple of suspects. One of them was your friend, Dr. Walker. I know they couldn't arrest any of the people from the consulate, but we will head downtown and see if we can get some information from the guys they took into custody. I'm not going in until tomorrow morning but I know they won't release them until I get there and have a chance to question them," he concluded.

"Well, we are all safe and sound here, and I'll be staying with them from now on," Phil said. "I'm going to send Carl out to get some groceries and then we'll get together tomorrow," I continued. "I know that there will be a major search for you guys," Tim said. "Do you think there is any way to trace you guys?" "I don't think so," I answered, but Carl will stay here with us tonight as well and we'll try and stay alert. "Ok, we'll see you tomorrow when I have a little more information.

I gave Carl the keys to my Uncle's Jeep and told him to go and get us something to eat. "Wow," he said. "I've never been involved in anything like that before. "That was pretty tense, and for a while there I thought we were going to screw up. "Well, it ain't over till it's over," I replied. "We've still got a lot of work to do." He took the keys and headed out the door.

I turned to the Velez family once more and returned to the couch and sat down by Selene. She had been telling her folks just what had happened and why. They began to thank me and asked what they could do to help. "There isn't anything we can do right now, but lay low until we can get more information," I replied. "Carl will be back with some food right away and we can eat, and then get you guys some rest," I continued.

"Come with me and I'll show you to your rooms," I said. We walked across the living room and up the stairs. The cabin was really quite big and very nice. My relatives lived here full time in the summer, so it was really more than a cabin. I showed the parents to their room and told them that Carl would buy them some toiletries. "But for the time being," I said, "just make yourselves at home and use whatever you need." There was a bathroom attached to the bedroom and I knew the couple would be happy with their accommodations. "I would like to take a bath," Mrs. Velez said. "That will be fine," I answered. "I'm sure you are worn out. My aunt and uncle leave a lot of clothes here, so just find what you can and wear whatever you like," I continued. "Come with me Selene, and I will show you your room."

Down the hall, on the same side of the house, I opened the door to her room. "It's not quite as fancy as what you are used to, but I hope it will be fine until we get this mess cleared up," I said. "It's perfect," she replied, as she walked to the window. I walked up behind her and we both looked out the window and onto the lake. The lights glistened off the lake and the moon reflected in the bay. "Are you OK?" I asked. "Yes, I'm fine, thanks to you," she answered. "You have been so courageous, and I'm so glad I trusted you. When I talked to you in the hotel room I really wasn't sure if I should listen or not, but my heart said you were for real and I'm so thankful I followed it." "I better go," I said. "And wait for Carl to get back." "Please don't go," she answered. Carl won't be back for a while so please just sit on the bed here with me and tell me about yourself," she continued. I sat beside her and as I did my knee touched hers. I had never felt anything like it in my life. I had many relationships in my life but I never felt a trembling like this before. I wondered if she had the same feelings but quickly brushed away the thought, because I knew I wasn't in her league.

We sat and talked for about an hour before Carl returned. I told her about my life and the fact that I had great parents who raised me. She could see I was sincere when I told her about my mom and dad and the fact that they had no idea if I was dead or alive, guilty or not guilty. She reached over and took my hand in hers and stroked it as we spoke. I learned during that hour that she was a very down to earth girl and that she was raised much as I was, in a loving family.

"Tim is going to arrange to get you and your parents out of here tomorrow," I said. "We are thinking maybe in a villa near the mountains where no one can possibly find you." "For my parents that will be fine, but I'm not going anywhere," she replied. "I'm in this till the end," she continued. "I'm now just part of the team!" "I'm not sure that is a good idea," I said. "It would be pretty hard to hide you," I continued. "What do you mean?" she said, looking up at me. "I mean, how do you disguise the most beautiful woman in New York?" I laughed. She turned a little red and said, "Thanks for the compliment, but I can dress down pretty well. Just wait till you see me in the morning with no makeup," she laughed.

Just then Carl arrived with the food and we all came down the stairs to the table. He had several bags of groceries and a bag of tooth brushes, soap, deodorant and other necessities. He also had a bucket of KFC and at that point we were all so hungry that we would have gobbled down anything.

After dinner we all sat in the living room and I told the story from start to end. The Velez's sat in silence as I unfolded everything that had happened to me over the past several weeks. After I was finished I asked," Where do we go from here? We know that this has to do with the bombings and the price of gas in the United States, but how are we going to prove this plot?" I asked.

"All that we have now is a kidnapping charge and I'm sure with their lawyers in Washington we have a long road to hoe." "Mr. Velez I asked, "Does anyone, other than the government officials in your country, even know you two were kidnapped and held hostage?" "Not really," Mr. Velez replied. "The agents who kidnapped us told my staff I had gone on a holiday and I didn't want to be disturbed. But someone on my staff was involved in the case," he continued. "And I'm not really sure who that is."

I told them that my partners would be here in the morning and we could figure out our plan of attack and where we would go from there. I also informed the parents that they would be moved somewhere really safe. "Where are you guys sleeping?" Selene asked. "We've got a couple of couches here in the living room," I said. "And that will be OK. We want to be alert in case anything strange happens tonight." The three of them came over and gave Carl and I a hug and then headed upstairs for the night. I knew it was going to be a long night for me because my mind was racing, trying to think about what the future held for us.

First thing next morning I heard a car pull up in front of the house. I grabbed my gun and headed to the window to see who was coming. I was relieved to see it was Tim and Lisa. "You are just in time for breakfast," I said. The room was alive with the smell of bacon and eggs and Lisa enquired, "Who is the cook?" "It's Carl. He is acting like a chef today," I laughed. "How did everyone sleep last night?" Tim asked. "Ask them yourself," I said, as we all turned and saw the others coming down the stairs.

I introduced Tim and Lisa to Mr. and Mrs. Velez and because of our meeting the night before they already knew who they were. "Good morning everyone," a voice came from the top of the stairs. I turned around and saw Selene coming down the stairs. I had to look twice because this certainly wasn't the girl I was with last night. "Looks like your aunt isn't a real blonde after all," she laughed. "I borrowed some of her hair dye this morning. I hope she won't mind. Besides you said you needed me to look different if I was going to help with the case," she said. "I'm not sure who you are," I replied. "But did you see a beautiful dark haired woman while you were upstairs?" "Very funny," she answered. "No problem," I said. "We have room for one extra for breakfast anyway."

Everyone seemed hungry and ate very well. A few minutes after we started, Randy pulled up and came inside. Any food left?" he asked. "There's an Egg McMuffin in the fridge that we saved for you," Tim laughed. "Sure, sit down," I said. "There's lots of food. Randy joined us and we all enjoyed Carl's cooking.

"Guess it's time for a team meeting," Tim said. "I have been listening to the news this morning, and the top story is about the Embassy. A few people were arrested and are awaiting pending charges," he continued.

"What are they going to charge them with?" Selene asked. "Oh, I gave the FBI and CIA quite a bit to work with," Tim replied. "Everything from kidnapping to espionage to terrorism and murder," he continued. "It's preliminary, but I don't think the judge will let them out on bail until we can get our evidence together."

"Do you have some good evidence?" Mr. Velez asked. "Well, we have the three of you and we have a motive," I said. "What we don't have is any evidence on who did the bombings and who masterminded the whole thing, but I think I know where we can find some evidence." "Where would that be?" Lisa asked. "I think it is time for Selene and me to check out Dr. Walker's office. Randy we are going to need some help from you as well. I'm sure by now it will be big news on campus that Dr. Walker has been arrested and it's going to be tough to get into his place. I've been in his office many times," I said. "And if his secretary doesn't recognize me, I pretty well know where he would hide anything of value. At least that is a good place to start. Once we are inside Randy can access his computer and e-mails and see if we can find anything that will help us."

"In the meantime, Tim and Lisa need to see what they can find on Mr. Zakari and his associates. I really believe he is the one in charge of the bombings," I said. "OK, we will head back to Lisa's office and see what we can come up with. In the meantime we need to get Mr. and Mrs. Velez away from here," Tim said. "I have a nice place reserved for you in Lake Placid and no one will ever find you there. Carl, take my uncle's jeep and take the Velez's up to the resort and stay with them until you hear from us," Tim continued. "Mr. and Mrs. Velez, you will not be able to contact anyone while you are up there and I mean absolutely no one. Do you understand?" "Yes we do," they replied as they nodded their heads in unison. "Just pretend that you are on vacation and that you have a chaperone," I laughed. "Carl, help them get packed and here's a package of information," Tim said, handing him an envelope. "There is a page of instructions and some money which should take care of you for the next few days. Keep your phone handy and I will update you on a regular basis."

We talked about each of the jobs that had been assigned and then we got ready to leave. Carl took the Velez's out the back, into the garage and into the jeep. Selene hugged and kissed them goodbye and in another minute they were on their way down the road. We then said goodbye to Tim and Lisa, and they also headed out the door.

DR. WALKERS SECRET

"Well Randy, I guess you are stuck with us," I laughed. "Now here is the plan to get inside of the Doctor's office I continued. Selene and Randy listened intently as I explained what was to happen and how it should work. We got our coats on and headed for the campus.

As we arrived, I told them both that Dr. Walker's secretary, Ms. Campbell, went to lunch promptly at noon and always arrived exactly one hour later. I recalled she was very efficient and never late. We walked into the building and up the old staircase to the second floor. When we reached the top of the stairs, I asked Randy to go see if she was there. He casually walked by and glanced through the glass as he strode past. He stopped a few feet from the door and gave me the thumbs up that she was there. It was five minutes before noon so Selene and I hid behind the wall at the end of the hall and waited for Ms. Campbell to leave.

As predicted the secretary was right on-time and headed past Randy, who was sitting on the floor reading a book, and toward the stairs. I watched through the window until she appeared at the outer doors of the building and headed for the parking lot. It was time to go to work and we didn't have much of it.

Selene took her place at Ms. Campbell's desk while Randy jimmied the door to Dr. Walker's office. In a matter of a minute we were inside. Randy went immediately to the computer and began to look for anything that looked suspicious, while I headed to his book shelves where I had seen him put some documents. We had been looking for a few minutes when we heard Selene talking to someone.

I peeked out the translucent window in the office door but couldn't see anything but the form of a male. I could hear the conversation and it went like this:

"Where is Ms. Campbell?" he asked. "I'm sorry but she felt ill and had to go home for the rest of the day," Selene answered. "Well, I need to get into Dr. Walker's office," he continued. He asked me to pick up a couple of things for him." "Well, I can't let you in," Selene replied. "You'll have to come back tomorrow." "Look lady," he said gruffly, "I drove all the way out here from the city and I need them today. Mrs. Campbell knows me and would allow me in," he continued. "Why don't you just give me the key? I will be only a few minutes." "I'm sorry," Selene continued. "I will get into big trouble if I did that, and maybe even lose my job," she answered.

"What's her number at home or her cell?" he asked. "I'll just call her and let you talk to her and let her give you permission to let me in." "I'm brand new here, and I really don't know where her number is, but if you come back in thirty minutes, I will find it, give her a call, and get permission to let you in. Would that be alright?" she asked. "That's fine," he said. "I'll go grab a coffee and be right back." He turned and headed out of the office and down the hall.

As soon as he walked out, I opened the door and asked, "Did he say who he was or what he wanted, Selene?" "No, but I wasn't sure what to do, so I thought I'd stall for time and ask you two what I should do." "Actually, this could be exactly what we needed," I said. "What he wants is probably the same thing we are looking for. When he comes back, just let him in and when he gets what he wants, we will take it away from him. You know, like Robin Hood, who stole from the bad guys to give to the good guys." I chuckled. "How do you propose to get it from him once he gets his hands on it?" she asked. "I'll think of something," I replied.

Just then Randy said, "I think I found something. I walked over to the computer and it showed some information about some bank account numbers." "How did you access that?" I asked. "Hey, it's my job to figure out stuff like this," he replied. "That's why they pay me the big bucks at Google," he laughed. "Can you copy that?" I asked. "Of course I can, if I have enough time to decode it," he answered. "Well, we don't have any time," I said. "That guy will be back in twenty minutes." "I'm going to download this on the drive I brought and once I'm back in the office, I'm sure I can figure out the encryption," he replied.

"What about that guy who is coming back?" Randy asked. "How will you get that stuff from him?" "Here's what we will do," I told the two of them. "Let him in the office, and when he finds what he wants, we will both come in and relieve him of his information."

Randy continued his work on the computer and downloaded what he had found. Selene walked down the hall and served as a lookout for the man to return. A few minutes later she returned and said, "He just got out of his car and he'll be here in a minute. Randy and I quickly exited his office and waited in the hall for the man to return.

A minute later he walked back to the office and asked, "Miss, did you get ahold of Ms. Campbell?" "Yes I did, and she said you could go into the office but I'm supposed to get some identification from you, and phone her back. Do you have something you can show me?" she continued. She could tell he was upset but he reluctantly reached into his suit coat and pulled out a card. Selene took the card and then picked up the phone and pretended to call the secretary. "I have a Mr. Terry here Ms. Campbell," she said into the phone. "Would it be Ok to let him in?" she asked. "Ok," she said, and hung up the phone.

She looked at the man and said, "It's Ok for you to go in, but I was told I must be in the office while you get the information you need." "Whatever," he said as he proceeded into the room. He then proceeded to the bookcase, pushed back a small opening which showed a small safe. He knew the combination and withdrew some documents and stood there looking them over.

Did you find what you needed?" Selene asked. "Yes. I think I've got everything," he replied as he closed the safe back up. "May I put those papers in an envelope for you?" Selene asked. "No, they will be fine," the man replied and headed for the door, only to be met by Randy. "Is there a problem here, Miss Ash?" he said, looking at Selene. "No, I got permission to let this gentleman in and get some information for Dr. Walker," she answered.

"Ms. Campbell called me from her home and asked me to drop in and see if everything was OK." "Oh, by the way, this is John, from security," Selene said. "Sir this will only take a minute, but I need to see some identification," Randy said. "I already showed her," the man said, slightly irritated. "Sir, it's only for the protection of Dr. Walker and yourself and it will only take a minute," Randy insisted. As he reached for his information Selene arrived with a large envelope and said, "Here is something to carry those loose papers in." She reached up and took them from his hand. Reluctantly he released the papers and watched her put them in the envelope. "I'll seal this for you," she said, as Randy looked at his documents. In five seconds she returned and handed the man his envelope.

"Everything looks fine sir. I hope we haven't caused you any problems," Randy said. "No, that's fine," he said, and walked out the door and toward the stairs. As soon as he started down the stairs Phil appeared from behind the wall and said, "Did you get his papers?" "Right here," said Selena, holding up an envelope that looked exactly like the one she had just handed the man.

"Let's get out of here," Phil said, grabbing the envelope. "There is a back way out of this building." We walked down the hall and as we came around the building we saw the man about to get in his car when he noticed Ms. Campbell walking toward him. He called her over and we could just hear him saying, "I thought you were sick in bed." "No," she replied. "I was just out for lunch. He ripped open the package and threw it on the ground, furious at what he found. He then started running toward the building as his face turned red with anger.

As soon as he entered the building, we headed for Randy's car. We got into the car and quickly left the campus. "What was in that envelope you gave him?" I asked Selene. "Just some tests I found on Ms. Campbell's desk," she replied. "I don't think Mr. Terry will get a very good grade from his superiors," she laughed. We got into the car. Selene and I jumped into the back and we sped off back to the lake. "Are you going to see what's inside?" asked Randy. "I think I'll wait till we get back to the cabin," I replied. I looked at Selene and said, "Was that enough excitement for you for one day?" "Yes," she replied. "But I'm glad I'm not his secretary on a regular basis."

THE REAL ESTATE SCAM

Meanwhile, Tim and Lisa had made their way back to the real estate office where she had once worked. As they entered the door Lisa said, "hi Katie, is Mr. Petrie in?" "Yes he is," she replied I'll get him for you. "I've missed you the past couple of days," she continued. "But it looks like this good looking man is taking good care of you," she smiled. "Oh sorry," she answered. "This is Tim and he's my new boss. Katie looked at her directly and winked, indicating that she approved. "You can go in now," Katie said, and she stood and opened the door.

"Hi Lisa," said Mr. Petrie. "How are you doing?" "Good," she answered, and then she introduced Tim. "What can I do for you?" he asked. "Well, first of all I wanted to tell you that Tim is with the FBI, and he is my new partner. I think it would be in your best interest if you sent Katie for an early lunch. Tim stood and showed Mr. Petrie his badge and said, "I think you should do as she says." "Alright," he said, and picked up the phone and buzzed Katie. We waited a minute for her door to close and then we were ready to begin. Mr. Petrie sat in silent shock for a moment and then asked, "What is this all about?" Then looking at Lisa, "Are you telling me that you were undercover all the time you were working here, Lisa?" he asked. "Terry" she answered. "It doesn't really matter what happened before when I was here. All that matters is what is happening now."

"Let me begin by telling you that you have been under investigation for some time, Mr. Petrie," Tim said. "And it seems you have a very good and clean record so far. I would advise you to answer our questions forthrightly and honestly. This will only take a short while." "Answers to what?" he replied. "Do you remember renting a downtown apartment to a law firm of Foreman, Hudson and Zakari?" Tim asked. "Yes I do," he answered. "Is there a problem with that?" "Well," Lisa said, "You rented that office space at several times the regular rate and they disappeared a short time later. Can you explain that to us?" she continued. "I think I have the right to call my attorney," he said as he shuffled in his chair. "No need to do that Tim interrupted. "We are not charging you with anything and you have the right to ask us to leave if you like. We know you are not involved in this crime and there is no law saying we can't charge you for what you did, but we simply need to know who you rented to and where we can find them," he continued. "I can tell you that this is part of an international incident, and if your name becomes involved, your life and your career could be in grave danger."

"At this point no one knows about this but the agents working on the case," Lisa said. "I've worked for you for quite a while and you have always trusted me, and all I'm asking is that you trust me now this one last time." "What do you need?" he asked, looking very nervous. "We need a copy of the lease, or information on who the person was who signed it." "Well, it doesn't look like I have any choice, does it?" he asked. "No, not if you want this to be over today and you'll never be involved again in any way concerning this case."

Mr. Petrie turned, opened his filing cabinet, and withdrew a file. "I had never seen the man who approached me about the lease. He told me it was a very sensitive project and his clients would be willing to pay a premium for the property if it was kept private," he continued. "When he offered me that ridiculous amount of money not to say anything, I knew there was something fishy. But I wasn't doing anything wrong so I made the deal," he concluded.

"How did he pay you?" Tim asked. "A money order," he answered. "Do you have a copy of it?" Tim continued. "Yes, it's in the file," he answered. "Is there anything else you have in the way of information?" Tim asked. "No, everything is in the file," he replied.

"Mr. Petrie, I appreciate you giving us this information and I promise you have heard the last from us, if what you say is truthful. Unlike the people who signed for this lease and asked you not to talk about it, we, the FBI, are informing you that if you tell anyone about this, you will no longer be exempt from prosecution by our office. Do you understand that?" "Yes I do. And I assure you I will not say anything to anyone," he answered. Lisa took the file and we headed for the door.

Once outside the office the couple headed out of the real estate office and headed straight for the car which was parked around the corner. "Do you think he will say anything to anyone?" Lisa asked Tim. "I don't think so," replied Tim. "He looked pretty shook up and I don't think he knows anything about this case. He's sure by now that you were working undercover all the time you were in his office. Let's just hope that there is good information in this file that will help us clear Phil and shed some light on the case," Tim concluded.

When Tim and Lisa arrived back at the cabin, the other three were waiting for them. "How did things go at Dr. Walkers?" Tim asked. "It got a little scary there for a while, but I think we've got some pretty good evidence and a few names that could shed light on what has happened," Phil answered. "It went well for us too. I'm not sure what we'll find in this file but let's sit down and see what we have come up with so far."

For the next few hours we looked through as much material as we could. Tim brought the information that Phil had set up on his wall back in the condo. From here on out it would be a matter of piecing together all the information from the different sources.

Let's go over what we know for sure and then add in all this other information.

1. We know that the bombings had to do with raising the price of the oil worldwide.
2. We know that there are people here in the U.S., Venezuela and the Middle East who are working together and that those involved stand to make billions.
3. We know that a number of U.S. government officials are involved.
4. We know that Dr. Walker is a major player, as shown by the bank accounts Randy has accessed and the list of associates we got from the file we took from his office.
5. We know that the person who rented the law building, and set up Phil, was the same Dr. Zakari who paid for the lease.
6. We know that his real name is Rizwan but he uses his Zakari alias while in America. It seems that he once worked as a legal counsel for the Saudi Princes and had a falling out with them.

7. We know that currently, Eduardo Palma, the director of the Embassy and Dr. Walker are in custody, awaiting charges of terrorism. We also know that the charges have very little evidence at present.
8. We know that Selene and her parents were kidnapped and held hostage while their oil company was taken over by government people in high places in Venezuela.
9. What we don't know is just how many people are involved in this conspiracy and who is heading up this entire campaign.

After briefing us on what we had accomplished, Tim informed us that he would be the one heading up the rest of the investigation. He said, "It is tough wearing two hats and feeling like I am being dishonest with my superiors back at the office. I want to be there when the rest of the questioning is done," he continued. "We have an interrogation set up for ten o'clock tomorrow morning with Walker, followed by one with Palma in the afternoon."

"I believe I have enough evidence that one of them will cave in if we offer them a plea. But the real secret is to get them into court in a trial setting that will intimidate them. At least, I will have a better idea of where to proceed after tomorrow," he concluded.

"In the meantime, I need you to find out where Zakari is staying. By now he is aware that he is being looked for by the CIA and will either try to leave the country or go into hiding. Phil, you are the only one who can identify who he is and it will take a personal ID from you without making contact. Lisa, you will have to be the bait. He is known as a womanizer and if we can find him, it will be your job to get him to where we can secure him".

"Randy, do what you can to find him without alerting your company that you are doing this for the CIA. Once you locate him, I have a plan to catch him that I think will work. From the information we got from Petrie at the Real Estate office we know that he frequents a couple of local night clubs. One in particular is the Flamingo, the place that Petrie met with him a couple of times. Randy, see what information you can get on that club and who frequents it on a regular basis and we may find our Mr. Z."

"Lisa, you might as well stay here tonight with the rest of the crew and I better get back to my apartment, because I have a big day ahead of me," Tim said. Lisa walked him out to his car and kissed him goodbye. I'm sure I was not the only one who noticed that they had become very close. In a minute, Lisa returned and the rest of us agreed it was time to grab something to eat and get some rest.

Carl had left us a lot of food in the refrigerator so I knew we wouldn't starve. "Lisa, you can stay in the same room as Selene. There are twin beds in that room," I said. "That's fine with me," Selene said. "I always wanted a roommate," she laughed. "Randy and I will stay in the other room across the hall from you."

Dinner was good. After it was over, I asked Selene if she would like to go for a walk. "Sure," she said, and walked toward the closet to get her jacket. I grabbed my coat and said, "We might as well walk down the beach. I know my way around because I've been coming here since I was a kid." "That sounds fine to me," she answered as we headed to the back door.

The night was cool as we began our walk down the beach. Only the sound of an owl and a barking dog broke the silence of the night. We had walked only a few yards when Selene reached out and grabbed my hand and pulled it towards her. Naturally I didn't try to pull it away from her, but instead pulled her head toward my shoulder. We walked for a couple of minutes without saying a word to each other. Once by the lake we came to a community park. "Would you like to sit down?" I asked. "Sure," she answered as we headed toward a bench overlooking the lake.

I didn't really know what to say as we sat down and Selene nuzzled up next to me. Was I dreaming or was I really sitting this close to the most beautiful woman I had ever known? We just sat there for a minute until Selene broke the silence by saying, "Tim and Lisa look like they are getting along pretty well, don't you think?" "Duh!," I replied. "They try not to show it when they are around us but it is pretty obvious that they really like each other."

"Do you think it is obvious how much I like you?" she asked, turning her face so it was only inches from my face. "Do you?" I asked. "I mean, really like me?" She reached up and pulled me toward her and our lips met for the first time. It was the softest, most beautiful kiss I had ever experienced and it lingered for several seconds before we broke it. "Now what do you think?" she asked. "Please don't do that, just one more time or quit it some more," I begged, as we once again kissed each other. "Selene," I said as we once again broke our kiss. "From the first moment I saw you in that hotel room, I said to myself that you were the most beautiful woman I had ever seen. Much as I tried throughout this entire time I have never been able to get you out of my mind." "Well, I didn't fall as quickly for you, especially when you held that gun up to me in my room," she laughed. "But I must say you have grown on me."

"We'd better get going," I said. "We have a long day ahead of us." "Ok," she said as I pulled her from the bench. We walked back to the house with our arms wrapped around each other, finally arriving at the back door. The others had gone to bed so I gave her another kiss and reluctantly let her leave me and head upstairs.

The next morning I received a call from Tim. He was just getting ready to interrogate Dr. Walker. "Did Palma agree to come over to the CIA office this afternoon?" I asked. "Well, he really had no choice in the matter, but he said he would be there. "Do you have enough evidence to keep them in jail for a couple of days?" I asked. "We have our ways," Tim said, "Don't worry, they won't be going anywhere for a while. When we are finished interrogating them we are going to charge Walker with treason and Palma with Terrorism. I'll also make sure we have a hearing scheduled for the next couple of days so they can sweat in a cell and think about helping us." "Sounds good to me," I replied. "In the meantime Lisa, Selene and I are going to see if we can find Mr. Z and get away from anyone else so that your CIA buddies can arrest him as well." "I'll call you after I've talked to these two thugs," Tim said. "Ok, I'll look forward to hearing from you in a while and thanks," Tim I replied.

THE INTERROGATIONS

After Tim introduced himself to Dr. Walker and gave him his rights, he said, "Let's get on with it."

Tim — "Walker are you aware we know that you are involved terrorist bombing in two countries and are because of your affiliation with the people killed in the incidents you are to be charged with treason?"

Walker — "I had nothing to do with the bombings and I am innocent."

Tim — "Are you familiar with the Velez family from Venezuela?"

Walker — "I saw them for the first time just before the Embassy was raided."

Tim — "So, you are telling me that you had no idea they had been kidnapped and were being held hostage?"

Walker — "No."

Tim — "Do you know Mr. Palma, the ambassador from Venezuela?"

Walker — "Yes, he is an associate of mine."

Tim — "Did you know the Velez family was coming to the Embassy that night?"

Walker — "Not until I arrived there."

Tim — "Do you know there daughter Selene, and were you aware that she was also a hostage at the embassy?"

Walker — "No I did not."

Tim — "Let us show you a picture of yourself, Mr. Palma, and Selene Velez exiting the Limo a few days ago." He leaned over and showed him the picture. (At that point Walker began to shift in his chair and began to look uncomfortable)

Tim — "Do you know that any lies you tell us now will incriminate you later?"

Walker — "Well I was in the Limo with her, but thought she was a guest of Mr. Palma."

Tim — "For your information, we are interviewing Mr. Palma this afternoon. I hope he protects you as well as you are protecting him. Let's continue."

Tim — "Are you familiar with the name Phillip Chambers?"

Walker — "Yes, he was a student of mine in law school."

Tim — "Did you not recommend him for a job with the Foreman law group?"

Walker — "No I did not."

Tim — "Were you not his attorney and represented him at his hearing?"

Walker — "Yes I was, and he pled guilty to a terrorism charge and then he was sent to prison.

Tim — "Did he ask you to plead guilty for him?"

Walker — "Yes. He even signed the document that I presented to the court."

Tim — "So Chambers basically admitted his guilt, is that correct?"

Walker — "Yes. That is what happened."

Tim — "Do you know where he is now?"

Walker — "I believe he was killed trying to escape from the Northern Prison."

Tim — "Well, I talked with him before he disappeared into the wilderness, and his story is much different than yours."

Walker — "Well, it's my word against his and he now has no say, so I guess you will just have to believe me."

Tim — "He may be dead, but I have his story on tape, so now what do you think?"

Walker — "I've been in law long enough to know that his testimony will be inadmissible."

Tim — "Are you familiar with the name Zakari?"

Walker — "No I'm not."

Tim — "We have information documented that not only says you knew him but communicate by phone and e-mail, that you communicate almost daily and that the Chambers name was involved in those conversations."

Walker — "I still don't recognize that name."

Tim — "What about a Mr. Rizwan? Do you know him?"

Walker — "No. I don't recognize that name."

Tim — "Well, we believe he is the same person as Zakari and that they are both connected to you. Ms. Campbell was most gracious when we asked for information from your office. The fact is we have, in our procession, the information from the safe in your office, so I'm going to give you another chance to change your story and tell me why you were involved."

Walker — "How did you gain access to my safe? It's illegal and you can't use it in a trial."

Tim — "I was hoping that you would work with us and you would never have to go to trial."

Walker — "I think you are bluffing."

Tim — "Think what you want, but we have the Velez family and they are going to testify against you, so think about what might happen to you, your reputation and character before you decide not to cooperate with us."

Walker — "If I am guilty of anything, and I'm not saying I am, what are you offering me for my information?"

Tim — "I really can't tell you at this point, but it will be a lot better than what will happen to you if you don't come clean. I think I have enough and I will let you go for now, but consider what I've said and let me know if you want to talk some more."

Walker — "How long can you hold me here?"

Tim — "Think about it Walker. The charge is treason. You might just end up in that prison that you sent your friend Phil Chambers to."

Tim called for the guard and Walker was taken back to his cell. Tim then walked through the door to the observation room followed by agent Johnson who had been quiet while sitting in the room with Tim and Walker.

"What do you think, Kramer?" Tim asked. "Well, I recorded everything and I think he knows he's in a lot of trouble," he replied. "I need you two to keep this top secret. You are the only two people that have been involved in this from the very beginning."

"May I ask you a question Tim?" Kramer asked. "Sure, go ahead and I hope I've got a good answer for you," he responded. "It sounds like you believe that Chambers was framed and had nothing to do with that bombing. Am I reading you right?" "I got to know Chambers at the prison and I'm positive he was framed by Walker and whoever is involved. I doubt we will get much information from Palma," he continued. "He probably thinks he has diplomatic immunity and we can't get at him, but the kidnapping of Miss Velez occurred on American soil and I think we can keep him detained for a while."

"I tend to agree with you," Kramer said. "When are you going to question him?" "In about an hour," Tim replied. "Just make sure you get everything on audio and tape. We are going to need all the information we can get our hands on."

Interrogation Two

Tim opens with a few of the same questions that he asked to Walker after letting him know that Palma has already been charged with kidnapping, murder and terrorism against the United States.

Tim — "How do you feel with all of these charges pending against you?"

Palma — "I am innocent."

Tim — "How do you know the Velez family?"

Palma — "They are from my home country and Mr. Velez is one of our top business men."

Tim — "Why did you kidnap their daughter and hold her parents in detainment in Venezuela?"

Palma — "I was simply following orders."

Tim — "Orders from whom?"

Palma — "I do not wish to reveal this at the present time."

Tim — "But you do admit that you kept Selene Velez in confinement for the past few months do you not?"

Palma — "She was not a prisoner, but free to move around however she pleased."

Tim — "What about her parents?" asked Tim.

Palma — "They came here to see their daughter, and we merely provided a place for them to stay while they were here in the U.S."

Tim — "Their story is quite different than that, but you probably knew that."

Palma — "They may say what they want, but it's my word against theirs."

Tim — "What if I were to tell you that it is their word and also the word of your friend Dr. Walker?"

Palma — "I don't believe you."

Tim — "How do you know Dr. Walker?"

Palma — "We are just friends, introduced by a mutual party."

Tim — "Does that friend happen to be a Senator here in the United States?"

Palma — "I don't know what he does."

Tim — "Do you know a Mr. Zakari?"

Palma — "No, I don't know anyone with that name."

Tim — "How about a Mr. Rizwan?"

Palma — "No, I don't know him either."

Tim — "That's odd. He seems to know you. By the way do you know a Phillip Chambers?"

Palma — "I've heard of him because he was the one who set the bomb off in Dubai."

Tim — "Did you know of him before that occurred?"

Palma — "No that is the first I heard of him."

Tim — "We have secured e-mails and phone conversations from Dr. Walker which clearly show you knew of him well before the bombings."

Palma — "How long are you going to keep me here?"

Tim — "Questioning you? Not long. In Jail, hopefully for the rest of your life."

Palma — "I am an ambassador to your country and you don't have the right to keep me here."

Tim — "That's where you are wrong, Mr. Palma. The charges against you, as I told you at the first of this conversation, are for international crimes, some which occurred here in the United States. So the bottom line is this. You help us uncover this terrorist plot and we make a plea or you spend the rest of your life in prison. You are under oath and we have conclusive proof that you have lied several times. I am finished questioning you now, but you better think about what you have told me today and maybe reconsider some things. I can promise you that no one is going to stand up for you, and in fact it looks like you are the one who is going to take the biggest fall."

"Take him back to his cell agent Johnson," Tim said as he walked to the door. "Let me know if you want to talk again, Mr. Palma. I will be looking forward to seeing you soon," Tim concluded.

Tim returned to the observation room where Kramer was waiting. "How did you think it went?" Tim asked. "He looked pretty shook up at the end," replied Kramer. "You may get more out of him than you expected." "I hope so," replied Tim. "If we can make him convinced that he is the one the others are going to use him as their scapegoat, we just might convince him to turn some evidence over to us. Only time will tell," Tim said. "But I've had enough for now, so I will see you two tomorrow," he concluded, and walked out the door.

Once outside and in his car, Tim called Phil to tell him how it went. "How long will you be?" asked Phil. "I'm on my way right now. How do things look for tonight?" he asked. "We just got information that Zakari has reserved a table at the Flamingo tonight, and I'm getting that girl friend of yours ready to seduce him right into jail with the other two jerks. If we can get him arrested and questioned, I'm sure one of the three will turn on the other two." "I hope so," Phil answered. "See you in half an hour. Goodbye."

Zakari was one of the last pieces of the puzzle, and if we could get him into custody with the other two we felt like we could work them against each other. Lisa appeared from the bedroom in her disguise and she looked completely sensual. Her low cut bright red dress and the slit up her skirt looked extremely sexy. "What do you think of my creation?" Selene asked as she followed Lisa out of the room?" Tim heard her as he came through the door and said, "I'm not sure I like it that much, unless she was dressed for my eyes only." "Let's put it this way," Phil said. "I think Mr. Z will like it a lot. I would really like to be there but I guess if he recognizes me, it's all over," he continued. "You are right," Tim said. "This is a job for Lisa and I, because he very possibly would recognize Selene as well."

"That's too bad for me," Phil said. "I guess I'll just have to hang out with this fake blonde tonight and wait for you two to do your thing.

"Consider yourself. the luckiest man in New York tonight Phil," Selene interjected. "You must not realize that there are a million men who would give anything to be in your position tonight." "OK," replied Phil. "I will keep you company if you think you can handle a real man!" "Very funny," she laughed.

THE SEDUCTION

Tim and Lisa left the condo, got in the escalade and headed for the Flamingo. They knew they had to enter separately. Tim was the first to enter and got a table in the corner facing the bar. Lisa entered a few minutes later and took a seat at the bar. Tim nervously looked at his watch every few minutes waiting for Mr. Z to arrive. He had no idea what Zakari looked like, except for a brief description from Lisa and Phil.

Lisa seated herself so she could see the entrance to the nightclub, and so she could see Z when he arrived. Finally she held up her glass of mineral water to signal Tim he had arrived. He looked toward the entrance and saw him speaking with the hostess. She escorted him to a table a table just a few feet away from where he was sitting. He evidently came alone, but seldom left that way.

One of the cocktail waitresses came toward him and asked him if he cared for a drink. He eyed her up and down and then ordered something from the bar. It was time for Lisa to make her move. Slowly she got up from her bar stool and walked toward Mr. Z. She walked right by him but his eyes never left her as she walked toward the back of the night club. Once she was a few feet past, she stopped, turned and looked directly at him. She turned and walked straight toward him and said, "I know this may sound like a line, but don't I know you?" Z looked directly into her eyes and said, "I would never forget a face like that. Would you like to have a seat?" he continued. "Better look again," Lisa said. "I'm sure it was you who our company rented an office to a few months ago," she continued. "And I never forget a handsome face either. I work for a real estate company. Does that sound familiar?" "Actually I do remember you, but you look a lot different than the woman in the business suit who showed me that office a few months ago."

She slid onto the same side of the booth he was at and pushed him across with her thigh. "Are you meeting someone tonight?" she asked. "No, I'm just here alone to get something to drink and maybe a bite to eat. May I buy you a drink?" he asked. "No, I've already got one," she said, putting her water on the table. "By the way, my name is Lisa, if you don't remember," she said. "Oh, but I do remember," he replied. "Just call me Z," he replied. "Are you expecting some one?" he asked. "No, I just needed to get away from my boring real estate job," she continued. "Well, would you like to join me for supper?" he asked. "I had better not," she answered. "I didn't want it to look like I was coming on to you." "I would have felt flattered if you had done this on purpose, but since we are here why don't you join me?" he insisted. "That would be fine, if you are sure you are OK with it," she replied. "I'm more than sure," he said. "I would be honored if you stayed."

They ordered dinner and chatted for what seemed to be a very long time for Tim. She was careful not to look at him during the entire dinner. Finally she stood up and headed to the ladies room. Tim got up and followed her down the hall and around the corner. When he got to the corner, Lisa was waiting for him. "How is it going?" Tim asked.

"Why, are you jealous?" she replied. "Darn right I am, but what's happened?" "Well, I invited him over to my place for a nightcap, and he was eager to say yes. I told him we could go in my car and he thought that would be fine because he came by cab."

"Alright," Tim said. "I'll see you in the car and we'll continue with the plan." He turned and walked into the men's room while she waited a minute and then returned to the table where Z was seated. He paid the waiter and then stood up and helped Lisa with her jacket. They then headed out of the night club and toward the parking lot.

"Nice wheels," he said, as she popped open the door. "Hop in," she said. "I'll drive." In the meantime, Tim had climbed into the vehicle and hid behind the second seat. "How far do you live?" Z asked Lisa. "Just a few minutes away," she said. "I hope you have had a good time," she said. "I'm so glad I ran into you," he said. "And I'm glad you recognized me." Lisa had made sure that she had not talked anything about Z's business or what he was into. Instead they talked about where she was from and mostly about her background.

A few minutes later Lisa pulled up in front of the city jail and pulled over to the curb. "Why are you stopping here?" he asked. "Ask my partner," she replied, as Tim lifted his head from behind the seat. "Mr. Zakari, or whatever your real name is, you are under arrest for murder and terrorist activities concerning the Dubai embassy bombings," Tim said, holding a gun to his head. Lisa flipped the lock switch, and agents Kramer and Johnson opened the door exactly on cue. "Get out, and put your hands up against the car," ordered Johnson. "You can't do this," he shouted as Kramer frisked him. "I have my rights," Z continued. "All you get is Miranda rights," answered Johnson. "Cuff him. Let's get this piece of garbage into a cell where he belongs. Z looked back at Lisa and spit at her. Tim saw it happen and wanted to punch him in the face, but Lisa grabbed his arm and said, "It's OK, we got him."

Tim and Lisa came crashing through the door, excited about what had happened. Phil and Selena tried to look composed, as they tried to adjust their hair and clothes when the couple burst in. "Did you get him?" asked Phil. "Did we ever?" said Lisa, as they all met in the middle of the room for a group hug. "Tell us how it went down," said Selena.

For the next few minutes Tim and Lisa told, in detail, what had happened at the night club. "I can hardly wait to interview that scumbag," Tim said. "We still have a long ways to go to clear Phil, but we are much closer than we have ever been. I believe I can get these three thugs to show their true colors and start ratting on each other," he continued.

"There's no room for us all to stay here, so Selene and I will head back to the cabin," Phil said. "Ok," said Lisa. Make sure you behave yourselves," she laughed. "Can we drop you off at your apartment Lisa?" asked Selene. "No thank you. I think I can find my way back by myself." as she winked at her new found girlfriend. Phil and Selene said goodbye and went out the door, then to the garage where they jumped into the car and headed for the cabin. "I hate bucket seats," said Selene. Things had seemed to go as well as possible for this unlikely group of espionage agents. Selene called Carl on the phone and learned that her parents were quite happy in their new hide away and from the people who had kept them captive. Selene's mother got on the phone and told her that things were going well. Selene said that she would be up to see both her parents very soon.

Tim arrived at work the next morning and began to interrogate Mr. Z. Many of the questions were similar to those asked of the other two prisoners. All Tim was trying to do was to get their stories mixed up so that the prosecution would be ready when the hearing occurred a few days later.

The media was confused with the story. They knew that the people in the Embassy had been taken into custody and by that morning knew Mr. Z was also in captivity. Because Tim was the lead agent in the case, he was followed by the media trying desperately to get a story. He continued to say, "No comment." But told them he would conduct a news conference the next day. The reporters were going crazy, because they could not find anyone else, besides Tim, who had anything to do with the case. Even Tim's superiors had no answers or how things had evolved. All they knew is that he was a good agent and they were going to back him on whatever his stand was. Once the news was released Tim knew that this would get major worldwide attention, and he also knew how important it would be to make sure he was well prepared to say the right things. Tim understood that several individuals from many countries around the world were involved in this story, including a few prominent people in the U.S. government. Tonight would be spent with the secret spies trying to decide how to introduce and handle the situation.

We all met at the cabin and began to talk about what Tim could say at the news conference. He knew that the lawyers for the defendants would be in attendance and would try to get all the information they could on the case. "Tim, it looks like you are going to have to say you solved this case on your own," said Phil. "I know that, and I don't want to play my trump card until the hearing," he answered. "I assume that's me," Phil responded. "You've got that right," Tim said. "Can I attend the conference?" Phil asked. "Afraid not," Tim responded. "If anyone recognizes you or knows you are alive, our case could go up in flames. Watch it on TV," Tim said. "I just hope I don't screw things up."

THE NEWS CONFERENCE

The conference was to take place in the chambers at court house. Tim really didn't know what to expect in numbers, but as he pulled into the parking lot he could see reporters from every part of the United States and other countries. He and Selene had to sneak in the back door and headed for the chambers. The room was completely full and Tim had never done this before. He took a deep breath and swallowed hard as he was introduced by the head of the CIA. He walked up to the mike, unfolded his notes, and began to speak.

"Ladies and gentlemen of the press and those of you interested in this case, welcome. I will give you all the information I can and I will not be taking any questions at the conclusion of my remarks."

"A couple of months ago there was a tragic bombing in Dubai. Several people were killed and more injured. No one took credit for the bombing, but a man named Phillip Chambers was accused of this crime. That bombing, and the one that followed in Kuwait, sent the world into mess and oil prices skyrocketed. Because Mr. Chambers was an American, as was the other accused bomber, there seemed to be a conspiracy against our Islamic friends from the Middle East."

"Mr. Chambers was taken into custody and sent to the Great Northern Prison in the far reaches of Canada to await his hearing and future trial. This was deemed to be the safest place for him at that time because of the volatility of the event. Mr. Chambers sought legal counsel from an old Harvard law professor who he trusted with his life."

"I was put in charge of the Great Northern Prison and was able to interview Mr. Chambers at length during his stay. I was also the one who informed him that he had pled guilty to all charges at his hearing by the same lawyer he had entrusted to his wellbeing. He emphatically stated that he never signed a confession and was in fact framed, and became the scapegoat of an orchestrated scheme. It was because of this that Mr. Chambers tried to escape from the prison. Many have assumed he was killed in the North Country, but even though his blood-stained jacket was found, his body was never recovered."

"Before he left the prison, he told me his story and those he thought were involved in the plot. When I returned to New York, I decided to examine the evidence and see if his story had any credence to it."

"What I discovered was an international plot, involving leaders of several countries and politicians, all interested in making millions of dollars by disrupting the flow of oil to the United States form the Middle East. As you all know, the price of a gallon of gas has risen to over $6.00 a gallon during the past month. I then tried to calculate who would benefit financially because of this catastrophe. That is when I met and was introduced to Miss Selene Velez of Venezuela and CEO of the largest privately held oil company in South America. I would now like to take a moment to let you meet Miss Velez, and have her tell you her story."

Tim motioned to the girl who was standing in the wings, waiting for her turn at the podium. She walked nervously to the mike and related the story of her kidnapping and that of her parents. For the next few minutes she spoke of how some officials in her country of Venezuela had set up this grand scheme and how they had threatened to kill her parents if she didn't do exactly as they asked. "They knew that if they kidnapped my parents that I would release the codes which would open our company bank accounts and give them full access to our family fortune. Our oil tankers were also seized, filled with oil, and sent on their way to America, as the price of oil skyrocketed in North America."

Once she had related her story, she returned to the back of the stage and Tim returned to the microphone and explained that his agents were able to free Miss Velez and her parents from the Venezuelan Embassy here in New York and put some of the potential terrorists in jail. He then announced that the family was safe and secure and in hiding until those accused of the plot were behind bars.

Tim finalized by telling the media that the CIA and FBI, working together, had three men now in custody, awaiting a hearing which should be in the next few days. "I cannot tell you their names, but I'm sure the bureau will have some information about them and their identities in the next couple of days. I wish I had more information for you, but as we receive further news we will let you know."

He then turned around and headed for the back door as the media tried to ask him questions. He grabbed Selene by the arm and headed for the underground parking lot, into his vehicle, and sped away from the Court house. Selene watched to make sure they weren't being followed and once they knew they were safe, headed back to the cabin.

Tim now knew that he and Selene were targets for anyone involved in this international crime. The day before the news conference, Tim had cleaned out his apartment, removed all the evidence he had gathered, and taken the contents to the cabin on the lake. Tim had also refused help from the body-guards at the Bureau. He told them that he had a secure location for all those involved in his group.

He knew that the courts would fast track the hearing and that he must lay low for the next couple of days. "Resting with Lisa would not be all that difficult," he thought with a smile. The couple returned to the cabin, put the vehicle in the garage, and walked in the back door. They were greeted there by Phil and Lisa.

"We saw the news conference on TV," Lisa said. "And you both did a great job." "Thanks," Tim replied. "I'm sure I looked pretty nervous up there." "Actually you looked very calm and in control," chipped in Phil. "Now we play the waiting game and hope we have enough evidence to keep those three in jail without bail until there is a trial. We need to stay hidden, because every newscaster in the nation will be looking for Selene and me."

Randy had arrived a few minutes earlier with enough groceries to feed us all for a week. "Randy, you have now become one of us, and I'm afraid you will have to remain with us here as well," Tim said. "You are going to be back in the spotlight again, because they have no other leads and there is a possibility that they will be looking for you as well. The most ridiculous thing is that the only one they are not looking for is Phil, because everyone involved thinks he is dead. That means that the only guy that can move around out in public is the very guy who got us all involved in this case." They all laughed.

THEY'VE FOUND US!

We all sat down and began to eat, when the phone rang. "This is Carl," said an anxious voice on the other end. "Let me put you on speaker," Phil said, as he laid his phone on the table. "Mr. and Mrs. Velez wanted to go for a drive, because we were all going a little stir crazy," Carl said. "When we returned, I noticed two men walking up the stairs toward our suite. I slowed down and stopped half a block down the road. I left the car and watched as they knocked on the door of our condo. The next thing I knew, they both drew guns from their holsters, and kicked in the door. I don't know how they found us, but I just jumped in the car and headed down the highway."

"When did this happen?" Tim asked. "Just five minutes ago," Carl answered. "Mr. Velez said he thought it was the same two guys who brought them from Venezuela to the States," Carl replied. "Just keep driving, but don't come back here," Tim said. "Where are you?" asked Phil. "I just saw a sign that said Bloomfield road a second ago," Carl continued. "I know right where you are," Phil said. "Exit off that main road when you get to Valley Ridge drive. There is a lodge about two miles up that road. See if you can get a room there. Tim and I will be there as soon as we can."

"Let's go Tim," Phil said. "We've got to get up there. Selene, you and Lisa stay here with Randy. We'll let you know as soon as we can what is happening." "No chance that is happening," replied Selene. "I'm going with you." "I'm coming too," chipped in Lisa. Phil looked at Tim, nodded, and said, "Let's get going." "Let me know what's going on," said Randy, as he laid his head down on the couch. "I'll watch the news and let you know what's happening," he yawned.

In a few minutes we were on our way to meet Carl. At least our phones were secure and we could still communicate. A few minutes later the cell phone rang. It was Carl and he said that they had secured a room. "Any idea how they found you?" asked Tim. "I think we solved that question," Carl replied. "We stopped to get a bite to eat this morning, and evidently Mrs. Velez purchased a trinket with her credit card. She just said it was automatic and she never even thought about it."

"Obviously, they have been monitoring everything they do, and it didn't take long for them to find you," said Tim. "It's a good thing you happened to take that trip after all." "I've got some pretty scared company right now," Carl responded. "We'll see you shortly." "Hang in there," Tim said. "We are on our way. By the way, what is your room number?" "214," Carl replied. "right on the second floor."

We sped down the highway with Tim driving the car. I sat in the back with Selene and I could see the nervousness in her face and her body language. I pulled Selene toward me and she rested her head on my shoulder. "It's going to be alright," I assured her. "Your parents are going to be fine. I knew that if the two body guards ever found Mr. and Mrs. Velez, they would kill them. With no one to testify of the kidnapping, our case would be very weak.

We were in the car for some time when I said, "Tim, Valley Ridge Road is just up the road on your left side. A minute later he made the turn and headed up the winding road to the lodge where Carl was waiting for us. We saw the lodge as we turned into the parking lot. Tim was careful to drive past the Inn before stopping at the far side of the building and scanning the area to see if anything or anyone looked suspicious.

"Phil, why don't you walk over to the office area and see if you notice anything unusual," Tim said. "Ok," replied Phil, as he opened the door and exited the Escalade. Tim picked up the phone and dialed Carl's number. "Hi," came the voice of Carl. "I saw you from the window as you drove in and I can see Phil walking towards us." "Have you noticed anything strange since you went to your room?" asked Tim? "No, only a couple of vehicles have pulled in since I called you," Carl answered.

Tim then looked at Phil and was given the thumbs up. He started back towards the room that held the frightened couple. Phil ascended the staircase and knocked on the door. Carl opened it and Phil motioned for them to follow him. They walked down the stairs where the car was waiting for them. Selene had crawled into the back seat and was soon joined with her parents. Phil and Carl climbed into the middle seat and Tim instantly headed back out of the parking lot and onto the road.

"That was an expensive room," Carl said. "But we are certainly glad to see you." "I guess it's time to get back to the Cabin where it all started," Tim said. "I just hope no one has made a mistake and they won't be able to trace us." I have a real bad feeling about this," Phil said, as they continued on their way back. "Where else could we have messed up?" asked Lisa. "I don't know," continued Phil. "But something tells me we are not out of the woods yet," answered Phil.

WE'VE BEEN COMPROMISED!

It had been a long day for all of them and they were all feeling tired as they arrived back in the city. "I'm going to drive in on the street just down from your relative's house," Tim said. "I'll drop you off here and you can walk to the cabin. I've been trying to get Randy on the phone ever since we turned off Valley Ridge road and there is no answer. "Alright," replied Phil. "Drop me off at the corner and I'll walk down and see if there is anything unusual. Just keep the cell on and I'll give you the all clear once I get inside. When you see the garage door open you will know that we are clear. Just drive directly inside and I will close the door behind you," he continued.

"Be careful, "Selene said, and reached out and stroked his arm as he slid out of his seat and onto the sidewalk. "Here is my gun," Tim said. "I hope you don't have to use it. Phil tucked it in the back of his pants and headed down the street toward the cabin.

The air was crisp, as the sun began to set on the lake. Phil took his time, and walked slowly down the sidewalk. He was startled by a small barking dog, as he came within a few houses of the cabin. Trying not to look conspicuous, he knelt down on one knee and called for the dog to come to him. The dog slowly came toward him and Phil reached down and began to pet him. All the time he was focused on the vehicles on the other side of the street, trying to see anything that might suggest he was being observed.

He patted the dog on the head and continued down the sidewalk. As he approached the cabin, he noticed a light on in the living room. He turned up the walk and headed for the door. A shiver went through his entire body as he noticed the door handle broken and the door slightly ajar.

Phil stepped inside and lifted the phone to his ear and said," Tim, we've been compromised." Tim reached under his seat and grabbed a gun. As he lifted his head he noticed a number of armed men moving toward the cabin. "You've got company," Tim yelled into the phone. "Get the hell out of there right now." "What about Randy?" Phil asked. "You have about thirty seconds before they get there." "OK," said Phil. "I'm headed for the boat house. Just pray my uncle's jet boat starts," Phil said. "If you see me motor onto the lake, meet me at the Jefferson City dock. It's on the north end of the lake. It will take me about five minutes to get there. You should get there before me."

Phil could hear the intruders approaching as he headed for the garage, locked the door behind him, and then down the enclosed walk-way to the boat house. Phil had grown up here and spent almost every day during the summers water skiing and boarding behind the boat. It was getting dark, but he knew he couldn't turn on a light without alerting the armed men who were looking for him. He reached behind the door and grabbed the key. "Yes," he thought to himself. "It's still there. Phil jumped into the boat, found the remote and opened the boat house door. At the same time he tried to start the boat's engine. The uninvited guests heard the boat trying to turn over and headed towards the garage. As soon as they found it locked they kicked at it trying to break the door from the dead-bolt that Phil had fastened.

"Please start," Phil thought to himself, as he reached down and pulled the choke. He knew he had only a few seconds before the hit-men would be coming through the door. Just then the engine started and Phil gunned the boat out of its stall and on to the lake. A second after he pulled out of the boat-house, he heard the door kicked open and the gunmen opened fire on him.

Two of the other gunmen ran down the lawn and began firing at him as well. He ducked down as the windshield shattered from the bullets of a semi-automatic rifle. He cut hard to the right and then back to the left, trying to make himself the hardest of targets. "Ten more seconds," he thought to himself, "and I will be out of range." He was crouched down under the bow as he heard a few more shots hit the boat. In a second the shooting stopped and he saw the gunmen head back for their vehicles.

Phil pushed his phone and said, "Tim, are you still there?" "Right here pal," came the answer. "We are on our way to the dock." Tim stepped on the gas and headed to the far end of the lake as fast as he could. "Those guys will be right behind you," Phil said. "I saw them heading for their vehicles as soon as I got out of range." "Ok," replied Tim. "We are only a couple of minutes away. If I beat you there, I will be on the boulevard waiting for you. One other thing," Tim said. "Throw that phone in the lake. I think they are tracing us. Mine is going out the window right now."

Phil turned off his phone and threw it into the lake. He could see the lights of the marina come on as he headed for the shore. He realized he had no time to dock the boat and headed for the beach. A minute later he could see the sand ahead of him. "My Uncle is going to kill me if he ever sees me again," he thought to himself. He slowed the engine down as he approached the beach. When he was within fifty feet, he turned off the engine and coasted to the shore. He ran to the back of the boat, lifted the motor out of the water, grabbed the key and jumped into the knee deep water as the boat hit the sand and came to an immediate stop.

It was about one hundred yards to the road. As he ran through the sand, across the grass and onto the parking lot he saw some headlights coming towards him. He prayed that they were friendly ones as he reached the sidewalk.

Tim steered his SUV toward a shaken Phil standing on the road. Carl opened the door and Phil jumped in to the vehicle. "We are out of here," shouted Carl, as he pulled Phil into the car. Tim gunned it and headed down the road. "Turn here," said Carl, and you will hit the highway at the lights." "Is there anywhere you haven't driven?" Phil asked. "A taxi driver has been about everywhere, and I make my money knowing the best way to get to places," he laughed.

"I didn't see any lights behind us," Selene said, as she looked out the window. She then lunged forward and wrapped her arms around Phil's neck and squeezed him tight. She rested her cheek against his and he could feel the tears from her face. Mr. and Mrs. Velez slumped together in the corner of the seat, with fear written all over their faces.

Tim reached up and pushed his on-star button. A voice said," On-star ready." "Call," Tim answered. "Please say the name tag, came a reply through the phone. "Kramer," Tim continued. "Ok, connecting to Kramer," replied the operator. The phone rang and a voice came over the hands-free phone. "This is Kramer," was the answer on the other end of the line. "This is Jones, and we have been compromised," he said. "I need the location of a safe house and I need it now," Tim said. "Yes sir," he replied. "I'll be right with you. I'll text you the directions," he replied. "Kramer, I don't know if my line is still secure. I will call you in five minutes and you can give me the instructions. "Yes sir," he replied. "I'll have it ready for you."

Tim and Phil looked at each other, both trying to understand how they had been discovered. "How did they do it?" asked Phil. "I don't know," Tim answered. "But everything is so electronically available now days that it's hard to hide anything. Interestingly enough Phil, the only one of us that no one is looking for is you," he continued, and you are the one who started all this. "So what is it like in a safe house?" Selene asked. "Well, there is no pool, if that's what you mean," he laughed. "Nothing elaborate," he continued. "But it is comfortable enough and you will be safe there."

THE SAFE HOUSE

Tim pulled the vehicle over at a convenience store, got out and headed for the pay phone. He was only on the phone for about thirty seconds when he returned. "Did you get the location?" Phil asked. "Yes. We are on our way," Tim said. "They will be waiting for us. About half an hour later we were driving into the country again. Finally we pulled into what looked like an orchard. We proceeded up a small road and finally what looked to be a small farm house came into view. It doesn't look all that safe to me," Carl interjected. "You shouldn't always trust your eyes," replied Tim.

We exited the car and were met by a young man who looked in his twenties. Tim was the first to exit the vehicle and walked over to him as we waited inside. After the two exchanged identifications, Tim motioned to us to get out of the vehicle and come into the house. Tim then introduced us to Brian. He was the safe keeper. We introduced each of the people and followed him inside the house.

Tim was right. The house inside was nothing like the outside seemed to be. We followed Brian to what seemed to be a little country kitchen, where he opened the pantry, moved a panel and pushed a button. Like magic, an area of the wall opened and a hallway appeared. Once again we followed Brian down the hall, where we went through an iron gate. On the other side of the gate was an elevator which opened and took us to our final destination.

"It's not anything spectacular," Brian said, as he walked us into what looked like an apartment. "You do have satellite TV and pretty comfortable beds, but these places were designed for short stays, not extended ones. How many of you will be staying?" Brian continued. "Just three," replied Tim. "just the Velez family."

"I'm not staying here," said Selene. "This is all about me and my family," she said. "If something happens to you, our case would be in jeopardy," answered Tim. "Why wouldn't you want to split up the witnesses?" she asked. "She's got a point," Phil said. "It might be better to separate them." "Maybe you are right Phil, but I think you have ulterior motives," he said smiling. "Not at all," Phil continued. "I really prefer women with dark hair," he laughed.

"Ok," said Tim. But we've got a lot of work to do, so let's plot out where we go from here. What are our priorities at this point? Let's make a list and see who should pursue each job." Brian brought out a white board and the group began the list.

1. Find Randy. Who knows if he is alive or dead? "I can find him if anyone can. I've been burning up inside ever since I found that door kicked in and saw no sign of him." "But how will you know where to look?" Lisa asked. "If he's got access to a computer, I can find him," replied Phil.
2. Put together the evidence. "Most of the clues we got I took to the bureau and I know they are secure. What we have to do

now is get together with the experts and analyze it so it can be presented at the hearing. Lisa and I can take care of that."

3. We need to get some information from the news networks on who else is involved in this plot. They have been on it for a while now, so someone has to have some info by now. "Carl, which role would you like to play next?" "I've been a cab driver, a chauffeur, a getaway car driver, a spy, a baby sitter, a chaperone, a target, a delivery man, a bell boy, and a cook. What do you need now?" he laughed. "how about being a reporter?" Tim replied. "I can you get you the documents to get into almost anywhere." "Sure," replied Carl. "Why not."

After everything was settled and Selene's parents were comfortably situated in their new accommodations, the group returned to the living room where they went over the details. Brian brought in four cell phones and distributed them to Phil, Tim, Carl and Selene. "These phones are completely secure, so you will able to stay in touch," he said. "Here is my number and if you need anything, just let me know," he continued. "If you need to contact your parents Miss Velez, just give me a call and you will be able to talk to them." "Thanks," she replied.

Brian then handed Carl a set of keys and said, "I've got just the car for you and it's parked in the back of the house. It looks like a regular Toyota Corolla but it has some real good features, like bullet-proof glass, an oil slick, on-star phone system and a Garmin. It also has some nice weapons located in the side panels of the back seat, just in case you need them." "Driving Tim's car around would not be a good idea at this point," he continued. "I know that you will need more than one car, but I'm sure they will have something for you at the Bureau."

"I guess it's time to go," Tim said. "Do you know where we will be staying?" he asked Brian. "Yes, it's a condo near downtown, with individual garages and an inside entrance. Here is the address. I just talked to one of our agents and it has been secured," Brian answered. "It has three bedrooms and a hide-a-bed. It is also equipped with surveillance equipment and the latest in computer technology. You will find some more guns hidden in the back of the closet including semi-automatic rifles and ammunition. Finally, here is some cash and a couple of credit cards." Brian handed each of the men a few hundred dollars bills. "Now, that's what I'm talking about," exclaimed Carl, as he was handed his wad of cash.

"Looks like we better get going," said Phil. "It's been a long day, and we've still got a lot of things to get done." "Let me say good bye to my parents," Selene said. "I'll be right back." A few minutes later Selene returned with a small bag. "I'm ready," she said, but Phil couldn't help but notice her tear-stained cheeks.

The five-some headed out the door and climbed into the car. Tim got in the passenger side, while Carl took his familiar position behind the wheel. Phil opened the door for Selene and then climbed in the back seat beside her. She leaned her head down on his shoulder and he put his arm around her shoulders. Lisa also climbed in the back seat opposite Phil. She reached down and took Selene's hand in her own and gave it a squeeze of assurance. Carl fiddled with the gadgets on the dashboard and then pushed the GPS as they rolled out of the driveway and on to their next adventure. "Now, if this was only an Austin Marti, I would know what 007 felt like," he laughed.

An hour later they arrived back in the city and at the condo that would be their home for the next few days. Once in front of the building,

Carl pushed the remote and the garage door opened. Once inside, they headed to the stair-case and then up to the apartment.

Carl keyed in the combination and the group headed inside. Once Tim scanned the rooms he invited the others into the condo. "Looks like everything is secure," he said. "Let's settle in and make ourselves comfortable." Carl checked the cupboards and the fridge and said, "It looks like I've gone from James Bond back to the chef."

There were three bedrooms, as well as an office, which housed the electronic equipment and a hide-a-bed along the back wall. Phil headed directly to the computer and said, "Excuse me guys, but I've got to try and locate Randy." "No problem," said Tim. "You get busy and I'll get everyone else situated. Phil instantly found Randy's private e-mail and typed in the following message. Phil knew that Randy could be a hostage, or worse, that he could be dead. As a result he had to be careful in his e-mail. His heart was sad as he thought of what might have happened to his best friend. Phil thought he would send the e-mail as if it was from Randy's parents and he used the old code that had always been theirs' alone. "Well, here goes," he thought to himself. His hands were shaking as he posted his e-mail:

Dear RANDY, Your dad and I were wondering if you are alright. We ARE worried because we can't reach you by phone and we haven't heard from you for over a week. Are YOU too busy to contact us? It's OK and we know you are busy, but I'm your mom and we need to hear from you. Love Mom and Dad. Phil pushed the send button and returned to the living room where the rest of the group was still talking.

"Did you send him a message?" asked Selene. "Yes I did. Now we will just wait and see if I hear back from him." "I hope he's OK. "Selene said, as she pulled him toward her and kissed him on his cheek. "We should know shortly," Phil sighed.

"It's been a long day, so we'd better get some sleep," Tim said. He glanced over at Lisa and she responded by saying, "We girls will take the master bedroom." "OK," laughed Tim. "We will see you in the morning." "I'll sleep on the hide-a-bed," Phil said. "I'm not sure I can sleep anyway, and I just might hear from Randy." As the two girls headed for the master, Lisa said, "Carl, I assume we will have an exotic breakfast waiting for us in the morning." "I'll see if I can locate something healthy for us. How about bacon and eggs?" he laughed. "I'll go shopping early tomorrow, so give me a list of what you need," he continued. "And I'll get you whatever you want."

It was just before 7:00 AM. Phil woke to the sound of the computer. He quickly pushed the inbox key and read the message as it opened up. It read.

Mom, I'M fine. Busy, and STUCK on assignment for a few days. You'll FIND everything is OK and I'll be home in couple of days. Believe ME, I'll tell you everything when I get home. Feed HILTON for me, he's a great dog and I never left him enough food. I'll CLOSE by saying I Love you—Randy.

Phil read the e-mail and then it dawned on him what Randy was saying. Phil walked to the bedroom door and popped his head inside as he knocked on the door. "Are you alone?" he asked. "Unfortunately, yes," he replied. "Come on in." "I think I found Randy. It sounds like he's alive and being held by the Cartel." "Do you know where they are keeping him?" Tim asked. "I think so," Phil answered. "I'm assuming it's a Hilton hotel near downtown." "Let me see that e-mail," Tim said. He walked over to the computer and read the message, turned to Phil and asked, "How did you get any answers out of that?" "It is a code we used when we were kids, and don't laugh, because it's the exact same code that I used to get out of your prison."

"If what you are thinking is true, why would they let Randy anywhere near a computer?" Tim asked. "Like I told you before, Randy is one of the best programmers anywhere replied Phil. I don't know how he did it either, but he is an electronic genius, so let's go find him."

Tim grabbed his phone, called the CIA office and gave someone all he had in the way of information. Tim told the person on the other end of the line to cross-reference Walker, Zakari, Venezuela, Oil companies and anything that had a Middle East name. Phil could hear the voice on the other end of the phone say, "Yes sir. I'll get on it right away, and e-mail you the information as soon as I get it.

"I'm having the office do a scan of everyone who has checked into a Hilton Hotel in down town New York and look for anyone who registered who sounds suspicious," Tim said. "Hopefully, it won't take long to get us a few clues."

Just then they heard the sound of the combination lock on the door. Tim drew the gun from his belt as the door began to open. As the person came into view, the men noticed it was Carl, with his arms full of Walmart bags. "A little help," he said, as they moved towards him and took a couple of the bags from him. "We didn't even hear you leave," said Phil. "I couldn't get back to sleep, so I took the list the girls gave me and headed out," answered Carl. "What did you get?" asked Tim. "You really don't want to know what's in a couple of these bags," Carl replied. "There's some girls stuff in there that I've never even heard of," he continued. "I just gave it to a lady staff member in the women's department and said my sisters told me to pick this stuff up," he laughed.

Lisa poked her head out of the door and said, "That must be for us," as she giggled. You couldn't help but see Carl turning a little red as he handed her the bags. He returned and said, "Hey, I did get us something for breakfast!" A few minutes later the women arrived and sat down to join us for some cereal, juice and muffins. "Nice matching sweats," he snickered, as he looked at the girls across the table from him. "Shut up," said Carl. "How did I know what to get them?" "Well, at least they are different colors," said Selene. "Besides, they are just fine. At least we got to shower and get cleaned up," she laughed.

Looks like you guys will be wearing the same thing you wore yesterday, including your underwear. At least we were able to shower and get dressed." "Look, I'm not that bad of a shopper," Carl said. "He reached down and pulled out from the bag three pairs of underwear. "They are all Joe Boxer," he said. "That's all I could find." "What did you say about matching sweat suits?" Lisa snickered.

The men finished off their breakfast and headed to clean up, returning about twenty minutes later. Tim called them together and said, "It's time to get serious and get back to work. We think we may have found Randy. He's alive, but being held by the cartel." He took a couple of minutes and relayed what had happened earlier that morning. "Memorize each of your cell numbers," he continued. "They are all the same, except for the last number.

Tim walked over and opened the back closet. "Here," he said to Lisa. "Put this in your purse." She reached out and grabbed the small pistol from his hand. She checked the bullets in the chamber and dropped it into her handbag. He then gave Selene, what seemed to be a little Derringer. "Have you ever shot one of these?" he asked her. "No, but I have shot a number of rifles," she replied. "This is simple, and you might need it if you get into a tough situation." He then handed her a holster with a belt attached. "This goes on your leg," Tim continued. "It only holds two shells."

Next he handed the guns for Phil and Carl. "This holster will fit nicely under your jacket, Phil, and yours can go in the glove compartment, Carl." Tim then looked at Lisa. "Have you still got their papers we got from the bureau?" he asked. "Yes I do," she answered, as she pulled some cards from the side pocket in her handbag. Tim took them from her and began handing them out to each of the group. "This is your ID. Use them if you ever get in a situation with the police or any other officers or agents. They are top secret passes and any law enforcement officer will recognize them."

"Wow," Phil said. "You look like you've done this before." "I have," answered Tim. "But never with a bunch of misfits like you." "Lisa and I are going to go to the bureau to find out whatever information has shown up in the past couple of days," Tim said. "You probably noticed an extra car in the garage. That is the one we'll take," he continued. "Carl, you head over to the New York Times and see if they have found out any more information on the story. I watched the news last night and I saw nothing on the case. I'm sure it's because a couple of the Senators are involved and the media has been told by the government to keep a lid on it until there is more information. Anyway, just dig up what you can, Carl. Just ask to see the editor when you get there and show him the pass I just gave you and he has to tell you all he knows or he could be sued. Oh, and go buy a suit before you go, there's a men's store right down the block from here."

"Yes sir!" Carl said, and saluted Tim at the same time. "Phil, you and Selene stay here and see if the office comes up with anything while we are gone. Oh, and you two behave yourselves," he laughed, as they walked out the door with Carl trailing close behind them.

Phil and Selene looked at each other and then came together, embraced, and kissed each other deeply as they fell onto the sofa. "It's about time we had some time alone," said Phil, as he pulled her on top of him. "What was that?" Selene asked. "You have got to be kidding me," said Phil. "That means there is a message in the in-box." "Well, aren't you going to view it?" Selene asked. "Oh my," he muttered as he slid out from under her and headed to the computer. "What is it?" Selene asked, looking over his shoulder. Phil read through the information and then said, "They think they may have found Randy."

FINDING RANDY

Selene pulled a chair up beside Phil and they began deciphering the message that appeared on the screen in front of them. It was fairly detailed, and gave several scenarios of three possibilities and percentages of which place Randy could be. "It's this one," squealed Selene, pointing to a Hilton near downtown New York. "How do you know that?" he asked. "Look at the names of the guests," she said as she scrolled back up the page. "See," she continued. "There was a room rented by Chavez oil. That is the name of my father's biggest rival in South America. It's registered under someone's name but if you look close, you'll see the visa card shows Chavez." "You are right," Phil said. "That's got to be it."

"I have a confession to make," Phil said. "And what would that be?" Selene asked. "You probably thought I fell for you because of you wonderful face, body and personality, but in actual fact I now know I fell for you because of your brains," he laughed.

"I've got to get over to that hotel right away," Phil said. "Get Carl on the cell." Half a minute later Carl answered. "What's going on?" Carl asked. "Where are you?" Phil asked. "I'm just down the street, trying on a suit," he replied. "In actual fact I'm in the dressing room standing in my new Joe Boxer underwear. "Well, I need you back here ASAP, but make sure you put your pants on before you leave the store," Phil laughed. "I'll update you on the situation as soon as you get here." He hung up the phone and called Tim.

The next call was to Tim and Lisa. "Hey, what took you so long to call?" asked Tim. "I think we've found Randy," Phil said, his voice almost trembling as he told them what had happened. "That's great," said Tim. "We are just about to the office. Lisa and I will try and verify everything you've told us so far. What is your plan Phil?" Tim asked. "Carl is on his way up here as we speak. He and I will go over to the Hilton and check things out." "That sounds good," replied Tim. "But be careful." "We will," answered Phil. "I'm going to leave Selen here. She can update us on any other information that arrives on the computer. Besides, she could be recognized," he concluded. "Would you see if you can access information on the room?" Phil asked. "Like how many are registered, if food is being delivered and maybe the layout of the room." "I think I can do that," Tim answered. "I'll text you whatever I can if we can find anything that will help."

A few minutes later there was a knock on the door. "Who is it?" Selene asked. "The boogie monster," Carl replied. She opened the door and let him in. "Where are we headed, and who am I supposed to be this time?" Carl asked. "I guess detective would be about right for you this time. Let's go back and pick up that suit," Phil said. "And I'll need one as well."

"Well I guess we are out of here," Phil said as he walked over and took Selene in his arms. "I'll text you and let you know what is going on," he said, and softly kissed her on the mouth. He then grabbed his shoulder holster and gun and followed Carl out the door.

Phil and Carl walked into the men's wear store and headed for the suits. "Oh, you are back sir," said the clerk, as Carl came around the suit rack. "Yup," Carl said. "Now where were we?" Half an hour later both Phil and Carl walked out of the store looking like two high class business men. "Do you have any idea what kind of a credit limit is on that government credit card that Brian gave you back at the safe house?" Carl Asked. Phil smiled and replied, "No, but I guess you will want to keep it after this thing is over."

They walked over, got into the car, and headed toward the Hilton Hotel where they hoped they would find Randy. "Let me off at the corner," Phil said. "I'll meet you in the lobby after you park the car in the underground lot. Make sure you park that car near the entrance so we can get out of here as quickly as possible." What if they don't have any good spots?" asked Carl. "Here," said Phil, handing Carl a hundred dollar bill. "I promise they will find you a good spot for a tip like that," he laughed.

Phil entered the lobby of the Hotel. He walked over near the fireplace and found a comfortable chair. He was pretty well by himself as he picked up the phone and called Tim. "Hi Phil, what's happening?" "I was wondering the same thing," Phil answered. "I just got inside the hotel and I wondered if you had located a room number. "Yes we have," replied Tim. Its room number 1886 and it looks like it's the penthouse." "That's Ok. I need to get checked in and see how close I can get to that room. Do you have a drawing of the top floor?" he continued. "It's on its way to your phone right now," Tim said. "It looks like there are four penthouses on the top floor." "I just got it," said Phil. "Call in and see what's available. If one of the penthouses is available then book it for me, and call me back."

In the meantime, Carl entered the lobby. He grabbed a newspaper and sat down across the room from Phil. Carl scanned the room and noticed a Hispanic looking man seated just a few chairs from him. He looked like a body guard he thought to himself. He pretended to immerse himself in the newspaper but was very conscious of his surroundings.

Phil heard the beep on his cell phone and looked over the email Tim had just sent him. He looked at the blueprint of the top floor of the hotel. He noticed that the doors to each of the penthouses were close to one another. He also noticed that each of the rooms mirrored one another, as he thumbed through his message. His phone rang a minute later. It was Tim asking if he got the layout. "Yes I did," Phil answered. "And were you able to book me a room?" "Yes. The adjoining room is available but only for two days," he answered. "It's under the Harper Corporation and everything is already paid for." "We are going to act fast if Randy is in that room. I hope you've got some idea of how to get him out of there," Tim continued.

Phil rose and walked towards the registration desk. "Yes Sir. May I help you?" asked the clerk at the desk. "My name is Ginger. I believe you have a reservation for me," Phil said. "What name is the reservation under?" asked the clerk. "The Harper Corporation," Phil replied. "Yes Sir. Here it is," she continued. "May I call a bellhop to assist you with your luggage?" "No thank you," Phil answered. "My bags got lost by the airline, but they said they will deliver them in a short time. Could you please give me two keys?" Phil asked. "My associate will be arriving in a short while." "Yes sir. Here you are. The penthouse elevator is the one on the far end. You must use your room key to activate it," she continued. "That will be fine," Phil said as he grabbed his briefcase and headed down the corridor toward the elevator.

Phil walked to the elevator and pushed in his card. The door opened and he entered, pushed the up button and the elevator took flight. In a matter of a few seconds the door opened and Phil walked out of the elevator. He noticed a man sitting in a chair outside of one of the suites. He saluted the man in the chair and got a wave back. He turned right and headed for room 1882, inserted his card and waited for the green light. It came on instantly. He opened the door and entered the suite without looking around. He walked forward toward the sofa, set down his brief case and walked to the window. He walked out onto the balcony and admired the view of New York. He then began an extensive search of the rooms to see if anything was tapped. After a few minutes he called down to Carl waiting in the lobby.

"It looks like everything is clear in the room," Phil said. "I need you to go to the staff room and find a bell hop uniform." "You've got to be kidding!" said Carl. "I've got to wear that little hat?" "I'm afraid so," Phil continued. "Just get suited up and then wait for Lisa to show up with my suitcases. Load them on the dolly and get the front desk to open the elevator for you. I alerted the girl that my suit cases would be arriving shortly. Her name is Ginger and she will assist you."

Once you leave the elevator, turn right and go to the only room on your left. It is room number 1882. There is a bodyguard sitting outside of 1886. Just ignore him and come right to my room. Have you got that?" Phil continued. "Yes I do," answered Carl. "In the meantime, I will call Tim and have him get the suitcases ready."

Phil hung up the phone and then called Tim. Phil told him how things were going, and asked if the suit case was ready. "I think I have everything that you will need to get things set up in the suite. There is an infrared camera, a printer and a laptop, some climber's ropes, a laser and a few other things that Lisa will take care of when she gets there. I'm sure that the guys in the next room are aware that you are there by now, but the cover for you is very good and not traceable," Tim continued. "Both suit-cases have false fronts in them, which have clothing in them. All the other items can be secured by the remote pen that Lisa has when she arrives with the cases. I'll call you back when she leaves my office. It will take her about ten minutes to get there."

Phil then called Carl and told him what was happening. "I've got the bell hop uniform and I'll head out and meet Lisa when she arrives. I'll see you in a few minutes," Carl said. Phil sat on the sofa with his hands covering his face. "Was Randy really next door?" he thought. He was about to find out very soon.

A Limo pulled up outside the Hilton and Lisa emerged from the back seat. The chauffer grabbed the suitcases from the trunk just as Carl arrived on the curb. "May I assist you with your bags?" he asked. "Thank you young man, that would be wonderful," she answered. Speaking of wonderful, Lisa looked amazing in her dress cut high up the thigh. Carl followed her like a puppy noticing that all eyes were upon her as she entered the lobby, especially the eyes of the man who she assumed was with the cartel.

Carl went to the counter and asked for Ginger. She said, "I am Ginger. Here is the key to the elevator." "Thank you," Carl answered, and then headed for the elevator with Lisa close behind. Inside the elevator Carl smiled at Lisa and said, "I'll bet that chauffer wasn't nearly as good as the last one you had," he laughed. "No," she replied. "But he was a much safer driver."

The elevator door opened and Lisa exited and headed for the penthouse. "Excuse me," came a voice from the man seated in the chair. He definitely had a foreign accent. He said, "I am security, and I need to see what is in your suitcases." "No one told me about that," Lisa answered. "But I guess it's for my own safety that you are here, so go ahead and look." She handed the keys to Carl and he opened the cases. The man took a look at the clothes and then said, "OK". Lisa gave a soft rap on the door as she inserted her card into the lock. Phil reached inside of his holster until he saw Lisa and Carl enter the suite.

"Wow! You look terrific," Phil said to Lisa. "Thanks," she replied. "I didn't want to look like an FBI agent. I've got all the equipment we need to get started," she continued. Tim showed me how everything works so let's get going. By the way, Tim has rented the room directly below us and will be here in a few minutes. Carl, go back down and help him get his bags to the room and then stay there and help him once he is settled in," she concluded. "Oh, and by the way, here is a tip," she said holding, out a dollar. "Very funny," Carl answered. "Not as funny as you look in that bellhop suit," she giggled. Carl smiled and turned toward the door and in a second he was gone.

Phil helped her with her coat as Lisa handed him the pen. "I'm going to change clothes," Lisa said, taking a pair of pants and a tee shirt from the top of the case. "I'll be right back," she said, as she headed for the bedroom. In a couple of minutes she reappeared ready to go to work.

"Let's unlock the cases and get out the equipment," Lisa said. Phil pushed the pen in and the lock popped open. He withdrew a number of items and placed them on the table. "What is this?" he asked, holding up something that looked like a video camera. "It's the infrared camera that will tell us if there is anyone inside the suite next door," she answered. "This is the power pack," she continued as she inserted the piece into the camera. "How does it work?" asked Phil.

"Simply hold it up to the wall and it will show you everything that is in the room," Lisa answered. "First we need to set up the printer so we can print what the camera shows us." Lisa plugged the small printer and monitor into the electrical outlet and turned it on. "Now hold the camera on the wall of the adjoining room and let's see what kind of a reading we get," she continued. Phil moved the camera slowly, up and down the wall, while Lisa watched the images on the monitor. "Are you seeing anything?" Phil asked. "Yes I am," she replied. "There are at least two people in the room. One is sitting and one has just entered the living room and is walking towards the other person." "Can you tell who it is?" Phil asked. "No. All the camera does is pick up heat and light," Lisa answered. "That way I can make out images, but I can't see any details. Take this and hold it up against the wall," Lisa said, as she removed another machine from the suitcase.

"It looks like a mini-satellite dish," Phil said. "Actually it's a sound dish, much like you see the guys carrying around on the football field," Lisa answered. "Hopefully we can make out what they are saying," she continued. Lisa then withdrew the head set from the suit case and placed it over her ears. "Can you hear anything?" asked Phil. "Yes but it isn't English, so I have no idea what the guy is saying," she replied. "By the tone of the voice and the fact that he just slapped the guy in the face, I can tell they are not best friends," she continued. "He's obviously trying to get some information out of the guy, but it's not working."

"It seems that the guy in the chair is tied up, because he hasn't moved an inch since we started. It's got to be Randy," Lisa said. "Wait a minute," she said. "He just asked him something in broken English. I'm not positive but it sounds like he wants information about the other agents he is working with. Oh my," she continued. "He just punched him in the face. We've got to get him out of there before they kill him." After a few more minutes the man left the room, leaving Randy tied to the chair.

"Take a break Phil," Lisa said. "Let's get an update from Tim." She grabbed her phone and called. Tim answered. "What's going on over there?" he asked. Lisa took a few minutes telling him what they had found out, including the fact that it had to be Randy inside the room. "Well, let's continue with the escape plan," he said. "Is Carl still in position?" he asked. "Yes, he's down stairs waiting to hear from us." "My guys here at the Bureau have all the information on the food that has been delivered to room 1886. I'm on my way to the hotel right now and I'll see what we can do to get something in the food for the guards in the room and in the hallway."

"Just an update for you guys. We have just been informed that the Cartel has contacted Washington and said they have one of our FBI agents held hostage. They said they are willing to make a trade for Zakari, Eduard Palma and Walker for Randy. It is becoming problematic for me in that Washington has no idea who the cartel kidnapped, and I can't tell them. I feel like I'm Robin Hood with my secretive little intelligence band. Bottom line is that we've got to get him out of there and as soon as possible. Once we get Randy out of there, the cartel will have nothing to trade with and the FBI will think it was just a bluff. See you guys in a few minutes," Tim concluded.

Lisa and Phil continued to monitor what was happening in the next room. For the next hour or so, they heard very little. Finally the phone rang again and it was Tim back on the line. "Hey, I'm in the room right below you," Tim said. "Phil, go to the balcony outside the master bedroom and I'll meet you there." "Ok," said Phil, as he walked over and grabbed the climbing rope, then proceeded to the adjoining room. He opened the French door and walked out on the balcony. He hung his head over the edge and saw Tim standing there. "Toss me the rope," said Tim. He hooked it around his waist and stood on the edge of the balcony railing. "I'm getting too old for this," he muttered. "And that is a long way down." He steadied himself as Phil and Lisa eased the rope through the pulley. In a matter of seconds Tim had pulled himself up on to the penthouse balcony.

"Why didn't you just come up the elevator?" Lisa laughed. "I'm the one person they might have recognized, and I wanted as little traffic in and out of this room as possible," Tim answered. "Now show me what you've got," he continued. Lisa led him over to the monitor and showed him the pictures. They listened to the muffled sound as well. "Looks like he's in there," said Tim. "And the best thing is that he's alive."

The phone rang again. This time it was Carl. "They've placed a food order and I'm going to pick it up in a few minutes," Carl said to Tim. "How much of this powder you gave me do I put in the food?" he continued. "About a teaspoon in each serving," Tim replied. "And then mix it into the food real well." "OK," Carl answered. "I'll put it in while I am in the elevator." "It will only take a few minutes and they will be sleeping like babies," Tim continued. Phil walked to the door and opened it just a crack so he could hear when the elevator arrived.

About ten minutes later the door opened and Phil could see through the crack that it was Carl. "Here is your food sir," Carl said to the man sitting on the chair. "Where is the guy who usually delivers the food?" the man asked. "I have no idea," replied Carl. "I just do what I am told. Besides, I have been assigned to this floor all day and it's not the first time you've seen me, is it?" "No, I guess not," he replied. "Just set it on the chair," he continued. "Yes sir," said Carl, and he leaned down and placed the covered plates on the chair. The man opened the top, looked at the food and said, "Ok, you can leave." "I hope everything tastes good," Carl said. "I'll be back to get the dirty dishes in a about an hour or so. Just leave them outside the door when you are finished."

Carl headed back to the elevator and opened the door. "Have a nice day," he said as the door closed. Phil could hear the man knock on the door and call to his partner. "Here is our supper," he said as the door opened. He handed some of the food inside the room. The door closed and the man returned to his post. He opened up the dish and began to devour it. Likewise, Lisa could see the other body guard sit down at the table and begin eating as well.

In the meantime, Carl entered the lobby again. By now he knew exactly who was watching him every time he entered or exited the penthouse elevator. He headed to the cloakroom and reappeared in a minute with a suitcase in his hand. This time however, he headed for the regular elevator. He ascended to the 17th floor and placed his key in the lock to the room directly under the Penthouse suite. He went straight to the balcony and called Tim.

"I'm here, Tim," Carl said, as he looked up at him from the lower floor. "How do I get up there?" he asked. "Just like I did," Tim answered. "Just climb up on the ledge, jump up and grab the balcony floor. We'll help you up." Carl looked down at the busy intersection and said, "Yeah right! No way, I'm doing that," he said. "I did it and you are a lot younger than me," Tim said. "You guys have had me do a lot of things and play a lot of parts but I'm no trapeze artist," he replied.

Tim turned away with a smile, then lowered the rope and harness down to Carl. "Very funny," Carl said. "Change out of that monkey suit and come on up," Tim said. "And make it quick. Carl disappeared into the bedroom and returned in a moment to the balcony. "Beam me up Scotty," Carl said, as he wrapped the harness around his waist. "We've only lost a couple of guys using this system," Tim said. "You should be fine." The three of them winched Carl up to their balcony and assisted him as he crawled over the rail. "I hate heights," Carl muttered, as he planted his feet on solid ground. Lisa and Phil quickly returned to their posts. "The guy inside is out like a light," Lisa said. "How about your guy down the hall?" she continued. "I can't see him from here," he answered. "Why don't you take a look, Lisa?" "Ok," she said. She opened the door and pretended to head for the elevator. She looked over and saw that the guard was also out cold as well. She turned and said, "Let's get Randy."

Tim walked out into the hall and Carl went with him. "Let's get this scumbag out of the way," Tim said. "There is a utility closet just down the hall. Put on these rubber gloves," Tim said. "We can't leave any finger prints." They opened the door and the two of them dragged the body into the small room. "How long will they be out?" Carl asked Tim. "Well over an hour," Tim replied. "It's a drug much like the date rape drug. They are semi-conscious but they won't be able to remember anything when they wake up." "Here is some duct tape," Carl said, reaching up on a shelf. "We might as well tie him up." "Good idea," replied Tim. "Maybe he'll get stuck here for a few days and he can see how Randy feels." "That's right," replied Tim. He then kicked the guard in the side with his foot. "What was that for?" asked Carl. "It was your idea to make him feel like Randy does when he wakes up."

By the time the two men returned, Lisa was already using the laser on the wall. "Let me take that," Tim said, as he continued cutting through the wallboard and a couple of two-by-fours." "It's amazing how powerful and quiet that laser is," Carl said, as the beam broke through the wall into the other end of the pent-house living room. Phil held his breath as they broke through the wall. He got a glimpse of a man sitting in a chair, facing away from him, but he instantly knew it was Randy.

It took a couple more cuts and the hole was big enough to get through. Phil was the first one through the wall. He headed straight for his best friend. Randy was gagged and had several bruises on his face, but as soon as the gag was removed by Phil, there was a big smile on both of their faces. While Tim untied Randy's, hands he heard the captive say, "Hey, what took you guys so long?" Once Randy was untied, the three men made their way back into the adjoining room. Lisa gave him a hug as Randy made his way through the opening in the wall. "Ouch! That hurts," Randy said. "Sorry," said Lisa. But Randy said, "Oh no. "It hurts really good!"

"Let's get things loaded up and get out of here," Tim said. Phil and Lisa repackaged the suitcases as Tim went to the balcony and lowered the rope down to the next floor. "Let me guess," said Carl. "I'm going out the way I came in?" "That's right," replied Tim. "You are first." Carl strapped on the harness and the others lowered him onto the railing. "You are next, Randy," Tim said. "We can't have anyone see you leaving the hotel." Once again they lowered the rope to the room below. "I'll take the suitcases with me," said Tim. "So when I get down to the balcony, send them down as well. "Randy, Carl and I will take the elevator down to the 2nd floor, and then take the stairs to the underground parking lot. Carl has the car waiting there for us. We will pick you guys up at the corner in a couple of minutes."

Phil and Lisa left the penthouse and headed for the elevator. The door opened to the lobby. When the door opened, the two of them headed for the front door. They walked hand in hand out, then turned left, and went down to and around the corner. Carl and the others were already there and the two jumped into the back seat with Randy. "You are a sight for sore eyes," Phil said to Randy. "Everything is sore, not just my eyes," he answered. "Let's get you to our new home and get you cleaned up," Lisa said. "is there any chance of getting a burger on the way?" Randy laughed. "Looks like the old Randy is back," Phil said as the car sped away.

When the crew arrived back at their condo, Selene met them at the door. "Oh my," she gasped, as she first saw Randy. She ran to him and hugged him close to her, as tears fell down her cheek. "What have they done to you?" she exclaimed as she looked at Randy's bleeding face. "Let's get him to the washroom and get him cleaned up," Lisa said, as she took his hand and led him away.

"You're not going to let those two girls get away from you?" asked Carl. "Not if we can help it," replied Phil, as Tim nodded his head. "But that hearing is set for 10:00 AM the day after tomorrow. We've got a lot of work to do between now and then to get ready," Tim said. "This has already been the longest day of my life," Phil said. "Do we have any five hour energy?"

Tim headed to the computer as Selene reentered the room. She saw Tim sitting in front of the computer and said, "Guys, I got quite a bit of information while you were out. The news said that the three men held in custody are demanding bail. If the judge grants it, I promise you will never see them again," Selene continued.

"I've got the greatest criminal mind in America prosecuting those guys," Tim assured the group. By the time we get finished with them they won't be going anywhere but to prison," he continued. "His name is Joe Earl. Lisa and I have been feeding him information like crazy for the past few days."

"Does he know about Phil" asked Selene. "He knows about everything including the kidnapping of your parents. We'll meet at the bureau tomorrow, so expect another full day. We will be leaving at 7:00 in the morning, so you guys and girls get some sleep," Tim concluded.

The next day was spent with Mr. Earl, going over in detail, all of the things which would be needed to keep these men in custody. After several hours, the group came to the same conclusions about the charges. Each man had been charged with a number of crimes and this hearing was to see just which were legitimate and which were not. After a full day the group returned to the condo exhausted and ready for the hearing the next day.

"At the end of the day it looks like Mr. Earl will use much of the following information to lock these guys up until a court date could be set," Tim said. "Here are some of the things they will have to defend tomorrow," he continued. "Internationally, they have all been charged with fixing of worldwide oil prices by creating a shortage using terrorist activities."

Mr. Zakari has been charged as follows:

1. Treason against the United States of America.
2. Murder in the first degree
3. Kidnapping of three individuals.
4. And a whole lot of other crimes

Dr. Walker has been charged with:

1. All of the above as well as falsifying documents about Philip Chambers.

Eduardo Palma has been charged with all of the above crimes as well as:

1. Using a foreign Embassy as headquarters for terrorist activities.

So, overall I think we have a good chance of putting these guys away for a long time," Tim said. "The most important thing is to find out who else was involved in this thing. I'm sure we can get at least one of them to spill the beans," he continued.

"Well, let's get some sleep," Phil said, as he walked over and kissed Selene good night. "That sounds pretty good to me," Tim said, as he laid a nice one on Lisa and headed up the stairs, trailed by Phil. "There is no way I am kissing Randy," laughed Carl, as he headed for the closet to get some blankets out for the sofa.

THE HEARING

The next morning came early as everyone scrambled to get ready for the hearing. The group left in two cars and headed to the court house. Tim and Lisa left first and took the attention away from the reporters on the front stairs, as Phil and Selene made their way to the underground parking lot. They were hurried into a small room with a large screen TV, where they would be able to watch the proceedings without being detected.

Meanwhile, Randy and Carl stayed in the condo and would have to wait until the foursome returned to get any real information on the case. They knew the hearing would be closed to the public, so all they could do was watch CNN and Fox for updates.

Tim and Lisa took their places on the front row right behind the attorney Joe Earl. A few minutes later, the three suspects walked in to the courtroom. Each was handcuffed and wearing orange jump suits. Phil watched, as the handcuffs were removed from each prisoner. He leaned over and said to Selene, "I thought I would never know what it would be like to be handcuffed, but I do and it was awful. Actually it does me good to see those guys tied up like that." "Not half as much as I do,"

Selene replied. It was odd for Phil, as he looked at two of the men he had once trusted and respected. Thoughts went through his head, as watched them on the monitor. "What people will do for power and money," he thought to himself.

"All arise," said the clerk of the court, as Judge Snyder entered the room. "You may be seated," said the Judge. "Let's get on with the proceedings. Remember this is a court of law. I would expect you in the media, who have been allowed to be here to witness this, will do so with dignity and respect during these proceedings."

The room was crowded with reporters from all around the world. This hearing was the headline in almost every paper anywhere. After all, oil prices had nearly doubled in America as a result of the killings and bombings that had taken place.

'The day of reckoning was finally here. In a matter of hours, everyone would know of the pending charges, and who was to be charged. The clerk of the court stood and read the charges for each man who stood to confront the court. When he was finished, the judge asked their attorney how they would plead on each charge. Each of the charged defendants stood as the charges were read to him.

Treason against the United States of America—not guilty

Kidnapping—not guilty

Murder in the first degree—not guilty

Many other less important charges were laid as well, to which the men plead not guilty.

The charges against Mr. Palma were a little different than the others because he was not an American Citizen. But they were still were very harsh. Phil couldn't help but notice that Zakari and Walker were both charged with falsifying documents, which lead to the capture and imprisonment of Phillip Chambers. It took almost a full hour to get through all the charges. At the conclusion, the judge said that he had reviewed the evidence for the past few days. He then indicated there would be a recess and that the hearing would continue in the afternoon.

Phil and Selene leaned back on the chairs and Phil said, "Well, I guess we're stuck here for a couple of hours." "That doesn't sound so bad, considering you have my company," Selene replied. After about fifteen minutes the door opened and in walked Tim and Lisa. "We brought you guys a sandwich and drink. It might not be that fresh," Lisa said. "But we can't have our ace witnesses running around out there looking for food." "They look just fine," Selene said, as she opened her juice box. Tim and Lisa then pulled some more sandwiches out of the brown bag and sat down beside them.

"Well, how do you think it went?" Tim asked Phil. "Just like I thought it would," he replied. "They are going to use a few tricks to get this thing thrown out of court, but I think Joe is ready for them." "What could they possibly use?" asked Selene. "Believe me, our country is getting a lot of pressure from governments all over the world," Tim said. "This case is a lot bigger than we ever thought," he continued. "Government officials from several countries are involved in this up to their ears. I think these guys are just the tip of the ice burg, and those guys lives are in great danger. They know way too much and we have them with security guards twenty four seven," he concluded.

The foursome visited for the next half hour, Tim and Lisa then returned to the courtroom. A few minutes later the court reconvened and Phil and Selene once again turned their eyes toward the monitor. "Let's get this show on the road," the judge said. "What do you have for us, Mr. Wright?" he asked the defense council. "We would like to have this case moved to a later date your honor," he responded. "What is your reasoning?" asked the judge. "We need more time to review the charges," Wright replied.

"I know this case is a little hurried, but you have had plenty of time to review the case, so the request is denied. Besides this is a hearing and not a trial," he continued. Mr. Wright returned to his seat and the Judge asked Mr. Earl to call his first person. "We call Mr. Zakari to the stand." Mr. Zakari was sworn in and the questioning began. Mr. Zakari you have been charged with some very serious crimes, yet you plead not guilty. So let's look at them one at a time," Mr. Earl said. "Let's start at the beginning.

"Last year you opened an office in downtown New York City, did you not?" "No sir. I did not," he replied. "You then hired Phillip Chambers, a newly graduated Harvard Law student to work in that office isn't that true?" "I know nothing of a law office and I have never heard of Phillip Chambers," he answered. "Besides isn't he the person who admitted to the bombing and killings and then died later trying to escape from prison?" "Just answer my questions, Mr. Zakari. We'll get to that soon enough. Isn't it also true that you were in Dubai the day of the bombing and that Mr. Chambers accompanied you there?" "No sir," replied Zakari. "I was in the United States the day of the bombing." "So you are saying that #1. You were not in Dubai, #2. You did not have an office in New York, and #3. you have no knowledge of Mr. Phillip Chambers. Can we enter that into the books, Mr. Zakari?" "Yes, to all three of your questions," he answered. "That will be all for now," Mr. Earl concluded. "You may return to your seat."

Mr. Earl then turned to the judge and said, "Your Honor, I would now like to enter some pieces into evidence which will clearly show that Mr. Zakari is lying to the court." "You may proceed," answered the Judge. Earl went to his desk and returned with a few papers in a large envelope. He took out a couple of papers and said to the Judge, "These pictures were taken from the office in downtown New York, where we believe Mr. Zakari set up his office. As you can see in the pictures, after we searched the office, we found residue on the window of the office, which when cleaned up, clearly showed the name Zakari and Associates, printed on the window of the main door. I would like this to be entered as exhibit "A" your honor." The Judge looked over the document, nodded his head, and gave a copy to the baliff to give to the prisoner's lawyer. "It is so entered," said the Judge.

"I would now like to call my first witness, your honor." "That would be fine. Have the witness sworn in," he replied. "I call Miss Lisa Conrad to the stand." Lisa stood from her chair and moved into the witness box. Once she was sworn in, Mr. Earl began his questioning. "Miss Conrad, did you work for the real estate company in New York City that rented the office space to the accused and his company?" "Yes I did," Miss Conrad replied.

"Do you recognize the defendant, and if so would you please point him out to the court?" "He is the man sitting right beside the council, Mr. Wright," she said, pointing directly at Zakari. "How do you know this man?" Earl asked. "I worked as a secretary in the real estate office, and I was the one who drew up the papers for the lease," she responded.

"I saw him when he came to the office for his visit with our owner, but I don't think he ever saw me," she said.

"Was there anything unusual about the lease?" Mr. Earl asked. "Yes, first there was no expiration date put on the lease and the monthly amount was over ten times the normal amount." "Had you ever seen other contracts like this one in your time at the real estate office?" Earl asked. "No I hadn't, and I thought it was most unusual at the time." "I have no further questions at this time," Mr. Earl said. "Mr. Wright, do you have any questions of this witness?" asked the judge. "No sir, not at this point," he replied. "The witness may step down," the Judge concluded.

Mr. Earl once again returned to the Judge's bench with another envelope. He opened the envelope and gave a copy to the Judge. The judge in turn handed a copy of the document to Mr. Wright. "In these documents you will find some e-mails, bank account numbers, data and names that will clearly show that Mr. Zakari and Dr. Walker were involved together in this entire scheme," Earl claimed.

Mr. Wright turned to his client, talked with him a moment and then said, "I object." "What is your objection?" asked the Judge. "Where and how did Mr. Earl get this information?" The Judge turned to Earl and said, "Is there a problem with this?" "No sir. It was given to us by a reliable source, who at this point would like to remain anonymous." "For now I will accept that and accept this information until I have had a chance to read it. Objection denied," he concluded.

Mr. Earl once again approached the bench and addressed the Judge. "Your honor, I have not yet introduced evidence of the kidnapping that we the prosecution, believe heavily involved Mr. Zakari. I would like to put the witnesses involved in the kidnapping on hold until the other defendants have been questioned." "I have no problem with that," the judge said.

"I would now like to call Dr. Walker to the stand." "Please come to the stand and take a seat, Mr. Walker," said the judge. Mr. Walker stood and approached the bench. Phil could not help but notice the strain on the face of the man he had once so trusted and admired. "Wow, he looks tired," Phil said to Selene. "He might be more scared than tired," she replied. "You know that his life is in real jeopardy," she continued. "Did you see the number of guards and the amount of security, as we pulled in? The best thing that could happen for the cartel is to somehow get rid of those three guys. "I agree with you. "Are you ready to take the stand today if the ask for you?" Phil asked. "I'm ready, willing and able," she replied. "The sooner this is over the better. Do you think they will have to have my parents testify?" she asked. "I doubt it," answered Phil. "I think by the time Mr. Earl gets done with them, they will have no chance convincing the Judge they are innocent."

By now Dr. Walker had been sworn in and the questioning was about to begin. Mr. Earl began by asking Walker if he had changed his mind about his not guilty pleas as a result of what he had witnessed over the last hour. He squirmed in his chair and then in a soft voice said," No." "Your honor, I would like to present a document as Exhibit "C" if I may." "Carry on," came the reply. Earl then pulled the document from his hand and showed it to the Judge. "May I show this to the defendant?" he asked. "Yes. That would be fine," the Judge replied, as Earl handed a copy to Mr. Wright.

"Do you recognize this document, Dr. Walker?" he asked. Walker took a minute and then handed it back to Mr. Earl and said, "Yes."

"Is this the document you surrendered to the court that included the signature of Mr. Phillip Chambers admitting that he was responsible for the bombing in Dubai?" "Yes, that is the one," he replied. "Is it true that Mr. Chambers retained you as his lawyer as soon as he arrived back into the United States?" "Yes, that is true as well," he answered. "Why do you think he called you and not someone else?" asked Mr. Earl. "I'm not sure, but I guess he trusted me because I was one of his professors at Harvard," he answered. "Is that his signature on the document?" he asked as he once again showed Dr. Walker the paper. "Yes, I believe it is," Walker answered. "When did he sign that document, and were you the one who administered it to him?" Mr. Earl asked. "I was," he answered.

"I have a letter here and a statement that was given to the head of security at the great northern prison saying he signed the document for you, believing it was to give you power to represent him, not put him in prison for the rest of his life." "He's a lawyer," Walker said. "Don't you think he would have read it before he signed it?" he asked. "Yes I do," replied Earl. "And as a matter of fact, I have the copy of the document he did indeed sign. We have had our best people at the FBI analyze this signature and in comparing the two we believe that the document I just showed you is a forgery." "Say whatever you want Sir, but Mr. Chambers is not here to collaborate your story," Walker countered. "OK, we will leave it at that for now," Earl said. "So let's continue on with something else."

"You plead not guilty to a charge of kidnapping, but we have documentation to show that you and Mr. Zakari had mentioned Chambers name before the incident in Dubai occurred. So obviously you knew Mr. Zakari before any of this ever happened. Is that right?" "Yes, I had known him as a friend and nothing more." "My, my, that is quite a coincidence, isn't it?" Earl said with a smile as he looked at the judge.

"Also we found the names of Selene Velez and her parents in the same documents," Earl said. "Do you deny that they were kidnapped?"

"I object," said the words of Mr. Wright. "No one has any evidence that a kidnapping occurred, your honor." "That is true," the judge replied. "I will delete that for the time being." "I have no more questions at this time for Dr. Walker," Earl said. "Then we will take a recess and reconvene tomorrow at ten AM" The clerk said, "All arise." and the judge walked into his chambers.

Phil looked at Selene and asked, "How do you think it went?" "I believe Joe is setting them up pretty well," she answered. "You know that tomorrow will be a big day for both of us." "I'm pretty sure Joe will be calling both of us as witnesses tomorrow," Phil said. "They may be expecting me," Selene said. "But when they see you, the whole world might go crazy," she continued. "Make sure you shave your beard and mustache tomorrow, or people still won't believe it's you." "I don't know," Phil replied. "I'm getting used to having it. I just hope my girl likes me shaved," he laughed. "I've seen your naked face before. I quite liked it then and I'm sure I will like it tomorrow."

Just then Tim and Lisa walked through the door. "So far so good," said Tim. "Tomorrow I think they may be falling all over themselves. Are you guys ready to leave?" he asked. "We've got a van downstairs waiting for you, so no one can see who you are. I think it's safe to return to the condo tonight. Carl will be down there to drive you home." "That's fine with us," Phil said. "But shouldn't we wait a while till there's no one around?" "That's a good idea," said Tim. "I'll make sure the garage is clear and call you when I'm ready."

Phil took Selene in his arms and caressed her on the cheek. "I really want to talk to my parents," she said. "I'm sure they are fine and safe," Phil answered. "You can call them when we get back to the condo." "Who ever knew that we would be involved in something this big?" she asked. "I can hardly wait to get back and see what they are saying on the news," Phil said.

Just then Phil got a call from Tim, telling them to come to the garage. The couple made their way down the corridor where they were met by a van with Carl in the driver's seat. "Hop in," he said. "I've always wanted to be a delivery van driver." "Let's get out of here," Phil said, as they crouched down beside the seats. Carl pulled out of the garage and onto the main road. He started out and then made three right turns in a row to make sure he was not being followed. "You can come up for air now," he said. "I'm positive we are clear." "What kind of a delivery van is this?" Selene asked. "I'm not sure, but it says Kandies confectionary on the side," he replied. "Well, where's the chocolate?" she asked, looking behind her.

A short time later the troop arrived back at the condo. When they opened the door everyone was already there huddled around the big screen. "Boy, are you guys popular," Randy said. "This case is all any of the networks are covering today. I recorded some of it, but it's really the same thing over and over," he continued. Selene went to phone her parents, while the rest of the group went over the events at the hearing.

"The way those defendants looked today, I just can't believe one of them won't crack and blow this case wide open," said Tim. "I think the most vulnerable guy is Walker. He looked like he was sick up there on the stand." "Yes, you can tell he's way over his head," said Phil. "It's amazing what greed can do to someone." "This case is going to take a long time, and the thing we need to do is get those guys locked up until we can get to the bottom of this," Tim said. "This case probably won't go to trial for at least a year, so we are by no means out of the woods," he continued.

"Hey cookie, what's to eat?" asked Phil. "I'm starving," as he smiled at Carl. "How can you be hungry after that gourmet lunch Tim and I brought you this afternoon?" Lisa said with a smile. "Very funny," Phil replied. "I think that sandwich is still in my throat somewhere." "I've got it covered," Carl said. "How's mac and cheese?" "Actually I picked up a few groceries this afternoon, and I make a pretty mean chef's salad. It will be ready in about ten minutes," he concluded.

Selene returned to the room and sat down on Phil's lap on the chair. "How are your folk's?" he asked. "They are fine," she answered. "They wonder when they can get on with their lives. They have been following the proceedings all day. They are very scared and my mom isn't feeling too well because of the stress." "Well, hopefully tomorrow things will be concluded and life can get back to normal," Phil said. "I'm not sure they will ever get back to normal again, Selene said. "I'll just be so glad when this thing is over."

"Randy, have you noticed anything or anyone suspicious today around the condo?" Tim asked. "No, I haven't seen a thing. I have watched the monitors all day and haven't noticed anything unusual. I will watch the first few hours and then someone can spell me," Randy said. "But we've got to have someone monitoring all night. The doors are really secure and we should be just fine, but I'm not going to take any chances.

"The fact is a lot of people and a lot of countries are involved in this mess," Tim said. "Before this is over, I predict there will be more bodies on the ground. This is a mega billion dollar money grab and these guys know a lot of people in low places," Tim concluded. "You will have armed guards outside your room tomorrow, Phil. Nobody should be able to penetrate the Court house because we will have a lot of fire power watching it."

The little group ate their supper, and then they watched a movie before getting ready to turn in. The two couples snuggled on the sofas while the other guys watched the monitors and did some work on the laptop. Once again the men headed to their rooms in one direction while the ladies headed upstairs to theirs.

Carl fixed a pretty good breakfast the next morning and the little troupe headed for the courthouse. Upon arrival, Tim and Selene were once again ushered to the waiting room. A few minutes later the judge arrived and the court was then in session.

"Are both counsels ready?" asked the judge. "Yes Sir," replied both of the lawyers. "Then proceed with your next order of business." Mr. Earl. "I call Mr. Eduardo Palma to the stand," Earl said. Palma stood up and took his place in the witness stand.

"Mr. Palma, how long have you known Mr. Zakari and Dr. Walker?" Earl asked. "I have known Mr. Zakari for a short time, and I met Dr. Walker recently," he answered. "You have been charged with a number of serious offensives, but I would like to concentrate on the kidnapping charge at first," Earl began. "You pled not guilty to the charge, but can you tell me if you knew the Velez family before you arrived in America?"

"Yes, I knew of the family name, because they own a large international oil company that originates in Venezuela," he answered.

"Have you had any contact with them since they were brought to America?" Earl asked. "Yes, we invited them to come to America and stay with us at the consulate here in New York." "Do you know where they are now?" he asked. "They left the Embassy several days ago and our understanding is that they returned to Venezuela." "So, you are telling the court that Mr. and Mrs. Velez were here of their own free will, and that at no time were they forced to stay with you?" Earl asked. "No Sir. They were free to come and go as they pleased," Palma answered.

At this point Tim smiled at Lisa and Phil, and Selene did the same. Randy had done a good job of showing that the Velez family, had indeed, returned to their native land. "Looks like they bought that hook line and sinker," Tim whispered to Lisa. Randy had used his computer skills to purchase the tickets, get the boarding passes, and sent three of his friends on a free trip to Venezuela, under the guise of the Velez family.

"Are you familiar with a Miss Selene Velez?" he asked. "Yes," answered Palma. "She came here to work as an advisor for the Velez's company. She was here on her own free will and choice, and we provided lodging and expense money to her while she was here," he continued.

"Was Miss Velez sent to Dubai at any point during her stay here?" Earl asked. "I believe she was. In fact, she volunteered to go, if I remember correctly." "What was the purpose of her visit?" Earl continued. "I believe it was to deliver some documents to another oil company which was interested in purchasing the Velez Oil Company," he answered. "Why her?" Earl asked. "She is the CEO of the Company, and was doing this on behalf of the family." "Thank you, Mr. Palma. I have no more questions at this time," Earl concluded. "You may return to your seat, unless your council has any other questions," the judge answered. "I have none, Your Honor," answered Mr. Wright. Palma then returned to his seat in the court room.

"I guess it's my turn," Selene said, as she turned to Phil. "Yes it is," Phil replied. "Joe is going to call you next to testify." She adjusted her skirt, gave Phil a kiss and knocked on the door. An officer opened the door and together they headed upstairs to the court room.

"I would like to call my next witness, Your Honor," Mr. Earl said. "That would be fine counselor. Proceed." "I would like to call Miss Selene Velez to the stand." The side door opened and Selene walked into the room. To say she looked stunning would be an understatement. She had dyed her hair back to its original black color. You could see and feel the buzz in the room as she made her way to the witness stand.

The court room was filled with reporters from around the world. Fox news, CNN and the major networks were there covering the hearing. You could see and hear the Ipads and cell phones go into action, as the reporters started to text their affiliates as to what was happening in the court room. The defense was the most surprised to see Miss Velez enter the room. All of the defendants looked at each other in disbelief as she entered. "I thought you said she was back home," Wright said, as he looked directly at Mr. Palma. "We had witnesses say they saw them get on the plane." Wright just shook his head and sat down on the bench.

The next thirty minutes were the most intriguing moments of the hearing so far, as Miss Velez recounted her story to the court. She told about how she had been kidnapped and held by her captors with the threat of death to her parents if she did not cooperate. She then told of her trip to Dubai and her meeting with Phillip Chambers, and the package which supposedly contained the detonator for the bomb that she delivered to him. Miss Velez also said that she had been forced to do this and that if she didn't her parents would be killed. She continued by saying that her parents had been held hostage while the events occurred. She concluded by saying that she and her parents had escaped from the Embassy with the help of the CIA and FBI, and that her family members were currently safe and in protective custody. When Mr. Earl finished with Miss Velez, he said he had no more questions and turned the witness over to Mr. Wright.

While this was happening in the court room, Phil had begun to get ready, by going to the washroom and shaving his beard. He put on his suit and tie, and got ready for the next step in the case. It felt strange, as he shaved the beard and mustache that had become his constant companion over the last few months.

Back in the court room Mr. Wright approached the witness stand to question Miss Velez. He began by asking if she knew any of the defendants sitting in the court room. "I know Mr. Palma from my stay in the Embassy," she answered. "And Mr. Zakari, I know as a result of my conversation with Mr. Chambers at the hotel in Dubai," she continued. "Do you have proof that you were forced to go to Dubai, and if you even met Mr. Chambers?" asked Wright. "No," she responded. "I don't have proof of that, but it did happen just as I said," she replied. "So, do you have anyone who can verify that you were there? anybody?" "No, I don't have anyone besides Mr. Chambers, who actually saw me," she added. "Well, if Mr. Chambers is your only witness, and he is no longer with us, then you really have no proof then, do you Miss Velez?" he responded." "Not without him I don't," she answered.

"So what we have here, your Honor, is a story from a witness, who in fact, has a great financial interest to win this case," Mr. Wright said. "She has admitted to carrying the case that detonated the bomb in Dubai and can draw no tie to my clients that would implicate in this disturbing scenario. So, if the prosecuting attorney doesn't have any more credible witnesses than this, I feel the case should be thrown out," Wright concluded.

"May we approach the bench?" Your Honor?" asked Mr. Earl. "Yes. Both counsels come forward please," he answered. Upon approaching the bench, Mr. Earl asked Mr. Wright, through the judge, if the defense council felt that this one small issue was enough to throw out a case of this magnitude. "Well, credibility is important here," the judge replied. "But Mr. Wright, we are talking about a number of charges here that are important to this case. What if I were to produce another witness that could conclusively prove that Miss Velez did, in fact, know Mr. Chambers, and truly did meet with him in Dubai?" "If you have another witness, by all means bring the witness forward," the judge replied.

Both parties returned to their seats and the judge took a moment to advise those in the court room what had just occurred at his bench. He then said, "Mr. Earl, call your next witness." "I would like to call Mr. Phillip Chambers to the stand," he said.

There was a collective gasp from the court room the second Mr. Chambers name was announced, and an agonizing pause as the door to the court room was opened. Mr. Chambers walked through the door, looking strong and distinguished. As he walked past the defense council's chairs all three of the defendant's, including their lawyer, dropped their heads to their knees in utter disbelief. Chambers stopped directly in front of the men and then turned to look right at them. He stood for a moment until both Walker and Zakari finally lifted their heads and sadly realized it was truly him. Chambers then turned and took his place on the witness stand.

"Well, are you really Phillip Chalmers?" the judge asked the witness. "Yes Sir," he replied. "I thought you were dead," the judge continued. "In fact, I believe almost everyone in this court room and throughout the entire planet thought you were dead as well." "not hardly Sir." "I am Phillip Chambers and the last time I checked I was alive and well.

By now the court room was really buzzing to the point that the judge hammered his gavel on the desk and said, "Order in the court." It took a minute for things to calm down as a few of the reporters left the court but, most remained to see what was going to happen.

"I object." said Mr. Wright, as he rose to his feet. This witness was never in the documentation submitted by the court to us." Objection denied," answered the judge. "I can hardly wait to hear Mr. Chamber's story, and I'm sure the rest of the world is too. You may proceed with your questioning Mr. Earl."

"Why don't I just let Mr. Chambers tell his story, Judge?" Mr. Earl asked. "You will find that if he is allowed to speak without interruption, the story will speak for itself. Mr. Chambers has been working in cooperation with the FBI and CIA for the past several weeks on this case. When he has completed his story, the world will finally understand the immensity of this case, which has affected the entire world. This case has caused contention around the world, caused billions of dollars to be stolen, people kidnapped, people murdered, and tremendous injustices to several individuals, and in particular Mr. Chambers." "That will be fine," said the judge. "Proceed."

A complete hush came over the court room as Mr. Chambers told his story. The entire audience listened intently as he unveiled what had happened, including his meeting in Dubai with Selene, and the daring rescue of her and her parents from the Embassy here in New York. The people in the court room hung onto every word, and soon began to realize the enormity of what was happening. It took quite a bit of time. The people in the court room listened intently to Chambers testimony. He didn't reveal everything, but enough for Mr. Wright and the accused to know they weren't going home for a long time.

At the conclusion of Chamber's testimony, the judge asked if Mr. Wright would like to question the witness. He simply said, "no. I have no questions." "Then the court is adjourned. I will let you know my ruling on the case in the morning. As for you, Mr. Chambers, I will release you back into the custody of the people you have been working with." Phil turned and fell into Selene's arms. In a matter of seconds it was a huge group hug. The judge turned and headed for his chambers, as reporters descended on Mr. Chambers and Mr. Earl.

"I'm sorry," Mr. Earl said. "We cannot talk to the media until the judge renders a decision. We will hold a press conference once the judge has finished his work. Please excuse us," he continued, as he led the group out the side door of the court room. Several officers blocked the hall from the media as the small group left the room and headed down the hall.

"Well, we've got to get you out of here without anyone seeing you, so it's back to the van for all of us." The parking garage had also been shut off to the public as well. They headed into the basement and then into the parking garage and piled into the van.

Don't you think some of the networks will follow this van?" asked Phil. "I'm sure they will," answered Tim. "But we've got that worked out," he replied. "When we leave in the van, we will go directly to the Kandies headquarters and once they see us go inside the compound they will leave. Once inside the warehouse we will change vehicles and leave via the other exit." "Sounds good to me," said Selene. "Let's get out of here."

The concession van pulled out of the garage and, just as Tim had said, a couple of vehicles followed it. Once inside the warehouse, the group transferred into a different van and in a few minutes they were on their way. A short time later they arrived back at the condo and pulled into the garage.

Randy was waiting as they opened the door and said, "You guys are the number one story all over the world again." He met Phil at the door and wrapped his arms around him. He said, "we did it buddy. it took a long time and a lot of work but we did it." "It smells pretty good in here," said Lisa. "What is it?" "It's Chinese food and there is lots of it for all of you. Dig in and eat."

Everyone was starved and they instantly dug into the food that awaited them. While they ate they watched CNN as it told the story of the bomb that changed the world and how a dead man named Phillip Chambers miraculously returned and closed the final chapter on the story. It was the lead story on every newscast and each of the reporters said that it was far from being over. There we rumors of government officials from several countries who were involved, but none of the names had been released, except for the suspects who were in the court room.

"It's a long ways from over, is right," said Tim, as he put his arm around Lisa and leaned back on the couch. "Tomorrow's decision will determine everything, but I think you could tell by the reaction of the defense council that they were cooked." "I hardly recognized you," Carl said, as he walked over and looked at Phil's clean shaven face. "Actually I'm glad it's gone," said Selene, as she ran her fingers up and down his face.

"So, where do we go from here?" asked Phil. "I think I can take care of the book work to secure your release tomorrow. Then it's time for a vacation," Tim said.

"Don't worry about the vacation," Selene said. "I've already taken care of that. My parents' yacht is on its way to pick us up in New York as we speak. In a few more days we will be on our way to the Gulf of Mexico. Anyone interested in a free vacation?" she laughed. "Do you need a captain?" Carl's voice echoed from the corner of the room. "As you know, I am a man of many talents," he laughed. "We wouldn't go without you, Carl," Selene answered. "Well, I believe that Tim is the only guy with a real job anymore, so I'm in," said Randy.

"What about your parents? Are they coming to chaperone?" Phil asked. "No chance," replied Selene. We've been chaperoned long enough and this time I want you all to myself," as she grabbed him and planted a long kiss on his lips.

"So let me get this straight," Randy said. "You two guys and your beautiful women seem like you might have a little more fun than us. I'm telling you right now that Carl is not my type." "Oh wait. Did I ever tell you that I have twin sisters, and they will be on the yacht?" said Selene. "Now that's what I'm talking about," Carl said, with a yell. "I hope they like us," said Randy. "Oh, you'll have a lot of fun with them. It may take a while, but once someone gets to know you two, you are really not as bad as you seem," she laughed. "What about you two?" Selene said, turning toward Lisa. "No way are you going without us," she said. "But before we go, we've got some shopping to do, girl." "How about you, Tim? Would you like to tag along?" asked Lisa? "Do you have anyone else in mind?" he answered. "Very funny," she laughed. "I can hardly wait to get you on that ship. Don't even think about going back to work. For the next while you are all mine," she exclaimed.

"I would like to call my parents. I'm sure they have heard the news. Is it safe for them to come out of hiding?" she asked. "Once the Judge makes his ruling tomorrow, they will be free to see you and return home," he answered. "Speaking of phoning parents, I should probably call mine," Phil said. "No one in the world would be more shocked than my mom and dad, when I showed up in the court room today. They have assumed that I've been dead for quite a while now and I feel so guilty for putting them through this ordeal." "There was no other way you could have done it," said Tim. I know they will understand and be ever grateful to have their boy safe and alive." "Here's the phone, Phil," Selene said, as she walked over to Phil. "You go ahead and call them. I'll borrow Tim's cell phone."

Phil took the phone and headed to one of the upstairs bedrooms to make what would be the emotional call of his life. There was a pause when his mother answered the phone. "Hi mom, it's Phil. I'm sorry I just put you guys through this," he said, as tears began to run down his cheeks. "I love you guys so much," he continued, as his voice cracked. "It's ok," his mother said back to him. "I know you would have let us know if there was any way in the world that you could. I've got the phone on speaker and here is your dad. "Hi son," he said. You know we never gave up hope that you were alive and we always knew you could never have done the things you were accused of." "When can we see you?" his mother asked. "I think after the ruling tomorrow, I can come home right away," Phil answered.

The conversation went on for the next twenty minutes or so, and then they said their goodbyes. Selene met Phil at the bottom of the stairs and wrapped her arms around him. "How did it go?" she asked. "It was wonderful to hear their voices again," he answered. "You just never realize how much you love your parents and appreciate all they've done for you until they are gone," he continued. "I'm just so glad I got a second chance. Did you get a chance to talk to your parents?" Phil asked. "Yes," she answered. "They are real excited to get out of that safe house and go home."

"Now that everyone has had a chance to call their families, I guess it's my turn to phone my uncle and aunt, and tell them how we totally destroyed their home and their boat on the lake," Phil said. "I'm sure they have terrorist or bomb insurance on that place." "Don't worry," Tim said. "The government will take care of their loss. "That's easy for you to say, but I'm still going get killed when they see that place!"

"Well, let's wait and see what the judge rules tomorrow," Tim said. "Then we can make some decisions on where our lives are going next. "What time do we have to be there?" Phil asked. "You don't even need to go," he said. "Just hang out here and I'll call you when he makes his decision."

Tim and Lisa left early the next morning for the courthouse. The rest of the crew just got up, showered, ate breakfast and waited for Tim's call. Finally the phone rang and it was Tim. "Put it on speaker," said

Selene, talking the phone away from Phil's grasp. "Is everyone ready?" Tim asked. "Yes," they all replied in unison.

"It will be on television in a few minutes, but I will give you the verdict first. The Judge ruled that all of the charges levied against the three defendants would be upheld until a trial date is set. Joe and I chatted with him after the proceedings. He said it will take at least a year for this to go to trial. Now get this," Tim continued. The three of them will remain in prison during that time with no chance of parole. They are to remain separate from each other during their entire time in prison. Now here's the best part ever he said. They are going to the GREAT NORTHERN PRISON!"

EPILOGUE
(ONE YEAR LATER)

After the story broke and the truth was given to the public, there was a surprisingly small outcry from the main street media. Mr. Zakari, Dr. Walker and Eduardo Palma all died mysteriously over the next year while serving their sentences. The countries overseas began shipping oil to America and the price came down. Once again big government in several countries denied any involvement and in a few short months those officials linked to the case were dismissed.

In my case, justice prevailed for me. But justice wasn't served and the corruption for greed and power continues throughout the world.

AS FOR THE CAST OF CHARACTERS

Carl was invited by Tim to join the FBI. He agreed and completed his training during the next few months. He currently works as an undercover agent and still reports to Tim on a regular basis.

Randy left Google and became a major programmer with the FBI as well. He currently works as the director of internet intelligence in Tim's office.

Lisa works harder than ever now that she has twins and a new husband, Tim.

They have one girl and one boy. Phillip and Selene!

Tim is a big wig in the FBI as well. He heads up a counter intelligence office with an international staff.

Selene remained CEO of her family's oil company and her parents retired. Her first move was to hire a competent lawyer, one Phillip Chambers, to oversee all the companies' businesses.

Phillip Chambers spends all of his time with his new boss and wife Selene, and loves every day of his life!

Edwards Brothers Malloy
Oxnard, CA USA
November 7, 2013